BELIN...
PASS...

by

ANONYMOUS

CHIMERA

Belinda – A Cruel Passage West published by
Chimera Publishing Ltd
PO Box 152
Waterlooville
Hants
PO8 9FS

Printed and bound in Great Britain by
Cox & Wyman, Reading.

BELINDA – A CRUEL PASSAGE WEST

Anonymous

'Do not be alarmed!' hissed the freak as he cupped her cheeks and stared into her wide eyes. 'Yes – I am a man! And because I need to dress as a woman I have been pilloried and run out of more towns than you could ever imagine!'

Belinda couldn't speak. Never before in her life had she seen or heard of such a thing.

'My nuns know what I am – and they still love me.' Once Salmacis could see she wasn't going to scream or struggle he continued. 'I see in your eyes great compassion, Belinda.' One hand slipped furtively to the back of her head and pressed so gently she barely noticed. 'I sensed it the instant I first set eyes on you. Do not forsake me out of ignorance. Do not forsake me like all the others.' As Belinda continued to stare confusedly up into the hypnotic eyes the other hand gripped the base of the rigid cock and aimed it at her slightly parted lips. 'Do not reject me, Belinda…'

Chapter One

Within minutes of Belinda landing in Virginia and meeting her wonderful new husband-to-be, he lay dead at her feet and the thugs who had stabbed him were advancing with intent to do the same to her.

Belinda's escape from a life of degradation and cruelty in Liverpool, her yearlong dreams as she awaited her journey to the American Territories of 1850 and her horrific voyage on a tobacco boat to Norfolk, Virginia, had all been in vain. Nineteen year old Belinda Hopeworth was now totally alone and helpless in a harsh and strange land, and was about to die a most horrible death herself...

Chestnut-haired, beautiful, with a full figure and a lively and intelligent personality, Belinda had had a happy life in spite of her mother dying from tuberculosis when Belinda was just thirteen years old. Her father and brother had run the family cotton clothing manufactory on the outskirts of Liverpool with sufficient expertise to enable them to live in a small mansion house in the suburbs, and all of Belinda's basic needs had been generously provided for.

But being of a somewhat independent mind, she had earned herself a worthwhile amount of pin money by giving music lessons. The fact that her father had been able to afford to buy her a grand piano and a harp had helped her little business enormously, and life for her was as near perfect as any life could be.

Her little world collapsed when first her father and then her brother had been arrested and imprisoned. The business had been struggling in the face of cheap imports from the empire, and her father, an otherwise honest man, had become desperate. He had started sending the same bills twice to his larger clients, and unfortunately for him, for a while their accounts departments had been paying him double for the same supplies. 'Unfortunately', because if he had been caught out at the beginning it would have been accepted as human error. But when a new office manager spotted and queried the double invoicing, it had not taken long to discover that this fraud had been going on regularly for well over a year.

Soon the bailiffs took possession of the elegant house and garden that had been Belinda's home, and, of course, her beloved and vital musical instruments. Within a few weeks she had been reduced to living in a stinking damp basement close to the River Mersey. Many clients abandoned her because her family was now classed as criminal, and those who stayed with her eventually faded away through natural wastage as the pupils achieved the required standard or became bored with music. She was a resilient girl, but in her reduced circumstances and with her family's black record, she found it impossible to acquire new clients and quickly approached desperation.

But luckily for her survival prospects she had another talent of which she was unaware. There was something about her pretty but tragic face that attracted certain gentlemen; gentlemen who had started talking to her as she wandered the dusty streets and had invited her to their drawing rooms to provide the particular services that they were especially interested in.

Virtuous in virtually every respect, Belinda had nonetheless allowed herself to lose her virginity to a horse groom when she was still sixteen. She was a sensual girl who often had strong sexual thoughts that could take over her mind, especially when inflamed by certain sights or sounds. However her very moral middle-class upbringing caused her to fight against what she guiltily considered to be her basest instincts, and she thus had an almost permanent struggle taking place inside her. The joy of her first orgasm had quickly given way to bitter feelings of shame and self-disgust, and she had vowed never again to do such a thing if she could possibly avoid it.

It had been a shock to her to discover exactly what these well-to-do men who invited her home were interested in, but her lack of other means had led her to accept the pain and humiliation that they had inflicted on her. What she found most heartbreaking was not the physical sensation, which she had started to tolerate very early on, it was the miserable amount of money with which the gentlemen – and in two cases ladies – had rewarded her. A half a day of being smacked, spanked, whipped, caned and, most horrible of all, indecently fondled, would only earn her just enough to pay her rent and buy her a minimal amount of food for half a week.

Her worst client had been a man who had a short cane made of stainless steel, specially manufactured for him by a famous firm of sword makers to his own design. Its lash across her soft white bottom was the most vicious agony, and afterwards when almost dying with the burning pain she had requested payment he had thrown her out with the utmost contempt. He shouted at her that she was a disgusting whore, and so low was she that he would no more think of paying her than he would think of paying a maggot-infested dog's turd.

7

Poor Belinda had fled that wealthy gentleman's city centre house in tears, and bumped straight into a man who was handing out broadsheets. Taking one from him by way of apologising for nearly knocking him over, she hurried back to her basement and read the small advertisements printed on each side of the coarse paper. She became more and more intrigued as she read, for all of the advertisers were gentlemen in America who were looking for English wives to join them. And from these she chose a natural-born American of thirty-five years of age with his own home and business in Virginia, an orphan who had made a decent life for himself, a man called Bill Wandle.

Their correspondence lasted a year, the return trip for each pair of letters taking around two months, during which time she had to continue to eke a living as best she could, which mainly meant playing the submissive role to clients who wished to strip her, beat her and generally humiliate her to their heart's content. She became partly inured to this treatment but could not wait for the day when she could set off for the magnificent new life that the wonderful sounding Bill was offering her.

At last the letter she had longed for arrived. Kind-hearted and considerate, Bill had arranged for her to take passage on a tobacco merchantman that plied directly between Liverpool docks and the small but bustling port of Norfolk in Virginia. He had done this at extra expense, partly to save her from the cramped filth and misery of the immigrant boats, and partly so as she would land closer to his home in Virginia, rather than having to go to New York as was normal with the third class passenger ships.

The four week trip would have been quite pleasant,

with few other passengers and plenty of room, if a thief on board, panicking at the prospect of discovery, had not chosen to hide some purloined trinkets in Belinda's bedding. The caning she had received from the bo's'n on her bare bottom in front of the rest of the ship's complement had been vicious but she had borne it stoically, telling herself it would be the last beating she would ever receive in her life. She did later have the pleasure of watching whilst the real thief – also a young woman – received the same punishment when she was finally caught. But what really stung Belinda was that nobody, from the Captain down to the passenger who had denounced her, offered the tiniest word or gesture of apology.

But all unhappy thoughts fled as she leant over the ship's side whilst it tied up amidst the bustle and the bales of cotton and tobacco at the Norfolk waterside. Bill, standing on the quay, had quickly identified her and had shouted happy introductions as he waited alone for her to disembark. She was relieved to see that he had a pleasant round face and was clearly as good-natured a man as his letters had implied.

She hurried down the gangplank as soon as it was lowered – her luggage was no more than her handbag and the full-length green and white dress and brown boots that she was wearing. Bill, abandoning all formality in his joy at seeing her beauty, had hugged her very full bosom tight to his chest, lifted her off the ground and swung her around, to the amusement of the roughly dressed but good-natured dockside loafers.

'Belinda!' he cried, 'I cannot believe my luck!'

'Oh Bill!' she cried back, her eyes swimming with tears of joy, 'I just know we're going to be so happy for the rest of our lives together!' She knew she sounded melodramatic but she was too happy to care.

She had also inwardly marvelled at Bill's strange accent, having imagined that Americans spoke like English people, but it was curiously attractive and added to his appeal.

'Honey,' he had called her, to her amusement, 'my carriage is just around the corner away from the port area. I've been waiting three whole days for you to get here and I had to station it somewhere out of the way. But it's all hitched up and the horses are rearing to get you back to my little old estate,' he cried out joyfully.

A few minutes later they were sitting up in his buggy and he was just about to take the whip from its holder when two big and very rough-looking men in torn leather clothes approached from out of the shadows and gripped the two horses by their halters.

'You ain't going nowhere 'less you all hand over your money now!' shouted one of them. 'So give it here and then you can get!'

Horrified and in fear of her life Belinda went to throw down her handbag which contained around twenty pounds in English money; her whole life's savings. But Bill stopped her.

'Just hold on there, honey,' he ordered in a firm voice. 'If we give into crime now then there's no future for America.' And with that he leapt to the ground and hurled himself at the nearest of the two thugs. The man fell backwards under the assault, but before the shocked Belinda could scream a warning the other man had run at Bill with a big knife. It flashed in the sun and Bill fell to the ground, clearly dead.

For a moment everything stopped. Belinda stared in shock at the cadaver of that wonderful man who had represented so much hope for her. But then the wheels of life started moving again and the two villains looked up at her. She screamed at them and threw her bag at their faces. They picked it up – but then started walking slowly towards her.

'Can't have no witnesses now, can we?' said the one Bill had assailed. His accomplice, the knifeman, grinned his agreement. They walked closer. In terrified desperation Belinda snatched the whip from its holder and with a simple double movement lashed both of them across the face. As they fell backwards screaming she continued the movement of the whip and cracked it over the horses' backs. Already nervous from the violence, they leapt into action and took off at an alarming speed up the hill and away from the port.

Just before they hurtled around the bend that would take them out of sight of the waterfront, the distraught Belinda looked back and saw the two murderers going through Bill's clothing and then dragging him to the bushes beside the road.

Almost blinded by tears of grief, disappointment and terror, she kept the horses at a flat out gallop for several hours until, rounding a sharp bend on a hillside, the buggy turned over after hitting a pothole. Belinda flung herself free but the buggy rolled over the side of the road and hung down over a sheer drop. It was threatening to drag the terrified horses with it but Belinda was able to free their harnesses. As the carriage crashed to the valley below the horses stampeded away and had soon disappeared from sight.

Now Belinda was truly lost, alone, penniless, utterly miserable and nearly three thousand sea miles from home. As she trudged tearfully down the dusty road her mind drifted. The life she had left behind suddenly seemed more appealing than this nightmare, she thought as bouts of mourning the murdered Bill Wandle alternated with the crushing disappointment

11

that her own new life was also dead and buried. She had never really minded the spankings and canings, she tried to convince herself, even if it did tend to involve a lot of unwelcome sexual attention. If only she had stayed in Liverpool.

A resilient girl, her spirits rose gradually as she tramped wearily along the trail, until they had bucked up to reach a level of mere numb misery. She then recalled her last visit to her brother in prison, when she had told him of her intentions of going to America, having told her heartbroken father the day before. But brother Charles had been happy for her, and had told her that they had an Uncle Albert who was well established in a town in California. It had a Spanish name which she couldn't remember, but she clearly recalled that Charles had told her it meant 'The Angels' in English. He said that Uncle Albert was a very enterprising type and would be sure to be doing well. If she had any difficulties she should contact him. Charles didn't know the address but said The Angels was a tiny town and she would have no trouble locating him once she reached there.

Now Belinda was torn. She knew from the maps of America she had studied whilst anxiously waiting for her husband-to-be to send for her that there were over two thousand miles of uncivilised land between her and the West Coast. But she also knew there were nearly three thousand miles of equally uncivilised ocean between here and Liverpool. With no money Belinda had no choice, and she staggered on towards the setting sun. If nothing better happened on the way, then she was California bound. And if there was nothing there for her then Uncle Albert could ship her home. And, she swore, she would never be ill treated by anyone again.

After another hour she had just passed a minor crossroads when her heart sprang into her mouth at the sudden thunder of hooves from behind. There was no cover alongside the road at this point and as she panicked a very expensive carriage driven by a highly aristocratic-looking man came to a sharp halt beside her in clouds of dust.

Dark complexioned, black-eyed and sharp featured, dressed smartly in black with a top hat, he beamed down at her.

'I say!' he cried, 'A beautiful damsel clearly in distress! My dear girl, do climb aboard and let's hear your story!'

And with that he jumped down and helped Belinda up. An experienced girl, she did not miss the significance of his patting her rather sharply on the bottom as she climbed aboard, but she had come to expect that sort of thing from almost every man she met.

He did not touch her after that though, and she poured out her sad story to him as they trotted along in the shiny black buggy. He showed great sympathy, and told her she must return to his tobacco plantation for the night at least. Very English, his name was Lord Raven and he claimed to be the biggest and the best slave owner in Virginia. He said he had maids and butlers, all Negroes, but if she was interested in staying on he would welcome an English housekeeper to run the household.

'But let's see how you fit in!' he shouted cheerfully as, at dusk, they drove through the arched timber entrance of his vast plantation and started the hour-long trot along his drive to the house.

Later that evening Belinda was delighted to find herself sitting with Lord Raven at his table, dressed

13

simply but decently in a thin floral-patterned low-cut gown that had been fished out for her from the loft. She was pleased at the way in which it showed off her full soft bosom to the best effect. The tobacco plantation's house was quite sumptuous and the dining room was beautifully furnished with a number of natural wickerwork and cane chairs and side tables. The large polished wooden dining table had a small banquet heaped upon it and she ate heartily of a refreshing fruit called a water melon followed by a choice of meats which included beef, duck and pork as well as boiled potatoes and cabbage – all very comfortingly British. This meal was luxury to Belinda after her recent experiences and Lord Raven was a generous and entertaining host. She felt more than just a surge of gratitude as she looked at him. In spite of, or perhaps because of, the suggestion of a sinister nature behind his handsome smile, Belinda could not help feeling greatly attracted to him, in an innocently romantic way. She kept pondering what her answer should be if he were to make any advances towards her. She hoped he wouldn't, because she suspected that she could be eventually persuaded, and she really preferred to avoid that sort of thing until she was married. His face was handsome if a little sharp-featured and autocratic now that she could see it in clear dust free light, but he had dressed immaculately for dinner in a black velvet jacket, patterned cravat and thin black trousers of an uncertain silky material, and there was little about him to repel any healthy young woman.

It seemed he had no family, and the only other person in the room throughout the meal was Wallace, the very dignified Negro butler, a large and comely man in spite of the grey hair at the sides of his bald pate. As he cleared away the remains of the meal, which had ended with some very nice cheese from the plantation's own farm, Lord Raven stood and poured Belinda and himself a French brandy. She had refused wine with the meal, not being accustomed to it, but she happily admitted to having a particular penchant for certain spirits and liqueurs. She had forgotten that she had acquired the taste from the groom who had plied her with such drinks before taking away her virginity in the stables back home.

Once Wallace had removed all traces of the meal from the long table, leaving only the pearly tablecloth in place, he stood back and coughed politely. Lord Raven consulted his ornate gold pocket watch and looked at the servant.

'Is Rosie waiting?' He asked Wallace.

Wallace smiled. 'Yes, sir.'

'Has she been waiting throughout the meal?' continued the master.

'She sure have, sir. And she know what to expect too, sir.'

'Oh excellent!' beamed Lord Raven. He saw that Belinda was a little puzzled but did not say anything to enlighten her except, 'You might enjoy watching this, my dear.'

Still unsure what was happening, she nonetheless managed a bright face of polite interest.

'Well, bring her in, man!' he said sharply to the kindly faced butler who immediately left them. He returned after a moment leading a devastatingly beautiful negress of around nineteen or twenty by her bare upper arm. In common with the rest of his lordship's slaves that Belinda had observed working on the estate when she had arrived, she seemed to be healthy and well nourished if not quite overfed. Her attire was easy to describe – barefoot, she wore a plain short-sleeved shift of thin black cotton that reached only halfway down her thighs. Her full round cheeks shone beneath the sparkling chandelier and she looked quite nervous, thought Belinda with concern.

Wallace positioned her before the master.

'This Rosie, sir, like I told you about.'

Belinda noticed Lord Raven's sharp eyes roam over the girl's full firm body, lingering where her large breasts pushed the black cotton tightly outwards. She didn't blame him, for Rosie was a very attractive girl.

'Rosie,' spoke her master, making her jump a little, 'Wallace tells me you don't want to work in my fields any more.'

Poor Rosie looked alarmed at that way of expressing her intentions and was about to reply but Wallace silenced her with a glower.

'But,' continued Lord Raven, 'that you would like to work in the house as a maid, replacing that idle sow Flower that I was forced to sell. Am I right, Rosie?'

The girl, eyes down, nodded and whispered, 'Yes master.'

'Now then, you can look me in the eye, Rosie; I want you to tell me what you expect to get out of working in the house. Don't be afraid.'

Rosie looked to Wallace for confirmation that this was all right, and he nodded.

'Master, I a good worker in the fields and all but I like to work in the house because I got the skills and the temperament. And also the house servants they get bit better food and much better beds.'

'But you know what else they get, don't you Rosie?'

'Yes, master,' she replied, lowering her eyes once again.

16

'Then tell my lady visitor what else you'll get if I let you be a maid.'

'I gets beat regular, master.'

'You get beat, Rosie. My slaves who work in the fields rarely get beaten, slaves are expensive and my neighbours who treat their vassals with too much violence and too little food find that they lose a lot of them both to disease from malnutrition and infected whip marks, and from running away. No slave has ever run away from my plantation, so I also save on guards as well. Ill-treated serfs don't breed so successfully either. But inside the house regular beatings are an essential part of my personal pleasure and therefore form one of my requirements.'

Lord Raven was addressing Belinda as much as Rosie. Belinda's heart was pounding a little at the scene that was being enacted before her, though she did not know if it were caused by fear or excitement.

'And you still want to be a maid even though you get beaten? The choice is yours, Rosie.'

Rosie nodded, her head down but her eyes raised to look at her aristocratic owner. He turned to Belinda.

'Well, my dear, you're in for a little treat. I know most women like to watch this sort of thing.'

Belinda was undeniably fascinated. She had a good inkling of what was coming, and it would certainly be a wonderful luxury for her to be a spectator rather than the victim. She also found Rosie's well-built body and shining skin coupled with her well-trained submissive personality equally intriguing. And she was just as breath-taken to notice, as Lord Raven stood up, that his tight-fronted trousers were bulging most impressively. Her toes flexed in her shoes and her thighs squeezed together as an instinctive reaction to her thoughts, reflexes that made her blush as she noticed them and

17

fought them down.

Lord Raven went to the grandfather clock and retrieved a barber's shop strop from beside it. As he turned around and both women saw the hard leather Belinda felt the flesh on her own bottom tingling.

The master stared at Rosie. He had the strop held in both hands across the front of his trousers, and Belinda could see he was pressing his penis with it, an observation she tried to ignore.

'Very well, my girl,' he said coldly. 'Pass this entrance test and you'll move in as maid this very night. Fail it and you'll be back in the fields at sunrise.'

Rosie brightened a little at that and nodded. Belinda was quite impressed to note such a simultaneous expression of joy and fear on a human face, but Rosie clearly felt confident about getting the promotion she wanted.

Lord Raven turned to Wallace who stood by impassively. He raised an eyebrow to the manservant, who immediately moved towards Rosie.

'How's sir having the girl?' he asked as he gripped her arms firmly.

'Let's try her as she is for starters, Wallace,' came the reply, and Wallace pushed her towards the nearest edge of the table. Standing tight behind her he pushed her down over the table and then went around to the other side to face her. He gripped her wrists and pulled them, her wide eyes staring into his. Her thin dress stretched tightly across her full bottom and rode up so that the top half of her thighs were clearly to be seen. As Lord Raven took up position sideways on to the girl, Belinda noticed with consternation that not only did the aristocrat have a whopping hard-on, but that the butler had pulled the girl's hands closer to him and had them pressed firmly against the front of his grey striped trousers.

Lord Raven asked Belinda to hold the strop momentarily whilst he removed his jacket, and Belinda felt its weight in her hands. About eighteen inches long, an inch and a half wide and nearly a quarter of an inch thick, the feel of it in her hands once again made the skin of her legs and bottom tighten as it brought back vivid memories for her. She was once again glad to be watching rather than receiving for a change.

The slave girl's owner retrieved the hard leather from Belinda, smiled at her and then wheeled around and cracked it into Rosie's bottom. The girl gave a shocked gasp as the crack echoed around the room. Wallace was still holding her close by the wrists, and her hands stretched out wide as a reflex reaction to the strop. Wallace beamed and pressed them in closer so that as they shut they automatically squeezed his bulging front and he rammed himself against her palms.

'Yes, very nice,' mused Lord Raven, 'but now let's raise the dress a little, shall we?'

Wallace released his grip on the girl, and the master made her straighten up. He then bent in front of her, took hold of her hem and pulled the dress up around her waist. Her full thighs and bottom were a very dark golden colour, Belinda observed as she watched with her breathing becoming faster and shallower.

Lord Raven beamed at Belinda's obvious interest, causing her heart to flutter romantically as she guiltily averted her eyes from the obscene but exciting display, and he then bent Rosie over once again. Her ample but firm buttocks stood up like great golden globes and the tightly stretched skin shone brightly beneath the chandelier. He looked at Wallace's trousers.

19

'You want your freedom, Wallace?'

Wallace grinned. 'I sure wouldn't mind, sir,' he said, and started to unbutton his fly.

The plantation owner turned to Belinda. 'He has a rather large penis, my dear. When it becomes aroused it can get caught up inside and cause him some distress which is no fault of his own. I trust you don't object?'

Belinda's eyes sparkled. 'I'm sure it's nothing I haven't seen before,' she said with a knowing smile and a shrug, her forced casual manner coming from a combination of wanting to impress this handsome nobleman and the increasing confidence obtained from the unaccustomed intake of brandy. Lord Raven leered lecherously down at her cleavage and then turned back to the table.

The butler finished undoing his buttons and reached in with his thumb and forefinger and pulled out his enormous erection. As it came free it burst upwards and stood there pounding against his waistband, very close to the prostrate Rosie's face. With a heavy sigh Wallace again took the girl's hands and made her grip his mighty black penis. Belinda was highly excited by now, and her hands dropped onto her lap, where she used the upper one to try to conceal that the lower was pressing as close as it could to her clitoris through her thin cotton gown. She had long ago found she could divert or diffuse her most sinful thoughts by complete or partial masturbation, and had indulged in this quite often as a safe alternative to real vice. She could see no moral wrong in this; even the Bible had only condemned the practice by men and had not mentioned women doing it. It was obviously a perfectly acceptable form of release from dangerous thoughts, especially as it involved no other person.

Lord Raven once again took up position sideways

on to Rosie. He closely examined her raised buttocks, stroking and pinching them both gently and cruelly. Then he suddenly thrust his hand fiercely between her legs and rammed it upwards to crush her clitoris with his strong fingers. Belinda was simultaneously alarmed and thrilled at this, and pressed herself through her dress again and tried to stroke the damp vulva hidden therein. She felt sure now that Lord Raven would try it on with her that night, and she was wondering whether to allow him access to her jealously guarded treasure as a precondition for marriage and the life of a lady on a rich plantation. As we will learn, Belinda's high morals were tempered by her equally high intelligence and the practical nature that came with being born into a factory owner's family.

Standing to the left of Rosie, Lord Raven raised his right arm. His free hand pressed the prominent bulge at his groin. He shifted position slightly and lashed the strop down so that it struck the girl's right buttock from the side. She screamed once and Belinda saw her hand jerk and crush Wallace's cock tightly. The butler thrust himself hard into her palm.

The master of the house then walked to the right side of Rosie. Standing square on to her bottom, he raised the strop above his head and then it shot downwards in a curve to strike her left buttock from the side. Rosie screamed and writhed. Wallace ground into her palms fiercely.

Lord Raven continued to strap the girl coolly and slowly, changing position and considering his aim between each stroke. He concentrated on her golden buttocks at first, but as they turned darker and darker he worked his way down the backs of her thighs to her calves. And all the time Wallace held her by the wrists and her hands gripped his gigantic baton.

In spite of her efforts to remain detached, Belinda was becoming overwhelmed by this fantastic scene, and was unable to prevent herself from masturbating quite blatantly through her dress while the men's attention was fully on the slave girl. She stopped dead, however, when Lord Raven suddenly turned and looked at what she was doing with a superior grin.

'I am delighted to see you are gaining so much pleasure from this, madam,' he smirked. 'If you are to stay here perhaps you should have a go as well? You will need to get used to it.'

Firstly covering her own unseemly masturbation by pretending she was brushing some crumbs from her lap, Belinda's heart pounded with terror. It was one thing to just sit and watch certain goings-on that one had no power to prevent, but to actively take a part was a rather different matter.

'I... I'm not sure I should...'

'Come, come, madam!' cried Lord Raven, his black eyes glistening above his thin smile. 'If you are to become a permanent part of this household you must surely learn to fit in with our ways, must you not?'

Belinda's heart once again thumped, but this time with excitement rather than terror. This extraordinarily sensuous man was either confirming his earlier offer of a position as housekeeper, in charge of people such as Rosie, or perhaps he was even hinting at marriage – into the aristocracy! She had to show that she could control staff in the customary manner.

Already full of suppressed desire, and her clitoris aflame from the near-orgasmic state she had brought herself to, Belinda needed no further prompting. She jumped up and snatched the strop from his lordship's hand before he could react. He and Wallace watched with joyful faces as Belinda gripped her hem from down by her ankles and pulled it right up so as to clench it between her teeth. She wore no knickers, and her marble white legs and thighs were fully exposed above her calf-length boots, as was her white vagina showing through her chestnut hairs. The dress held high, she proceeded to rub her clitoris fiercely, interrupting this every twenty seconds to aim at and lash the backs of Rosie's thighs until she screamed for her to stop. But Belinda, watched by the two delighted men, would not stop until she suddenly arrived at a long shuddering orgasm. When she opened her eyes she found both men and Rosie, who was now standing, staring at her. She suddenly felt extremely embarrassed. She could not believe she had behaved as she had.

Lord Raven chuckled a little sinisterly. 'Yes, very good indeed Belinda. But when I said it was time for you to have a go, I did mean to have a go taking it, not giving it.'

Belinda nearly died of shame and fright. But the whole electrical charge of the evening sustained her and she did not resist when Lord Raven sat her on the table and raised her dress.

'Rosie,' he said gravely, 'you are now a maid in this house, and Miss Belinda is a maid too. She therefore had no right to beat you. Her crime will be cancelled by you.'

Before Belinda could protest Rosie took the strop from her master, and as Wallace's arms encircled Belinda's waist and his hands slipped down to squeeze her vagina, the young girl got her revenge. She was cruelly unfair as she lashed Belinda with that wicked piece of hard leather, ignoring her screams and beating her thighs with a strength that Belinda had not used on her.

The pain was indescribable, relieved only by the black manservant fondling her clitoris, and it was not until after her legs were completely numb that the laughing Lord Raven dragged Rosie off and ordered her to her room; she was to be up at dawn cleaning and scrubbing the kitchen floor with cold water.

As the grinning girl left and the stinging subsided, Belinda's agony was replaced by a warm sexual glow, and when the Lord smiled at her and told her with a wink to go up to bed, she went willingly, infatuated as she was by that handsome and powerful man.

She lay in bed and tried not to masturbate in order to save herself for her new master's. She did not know that downstairs, after she had left the room, Lord Raven had smiled as he approached Wallace, and that Wallace had smiled back. The white master slowly pulled out his own considerable penis and grinned as Wallace took hold of it. He too gripped the butler's mast and they stared at each other as they mutually masturbated with long gentle strokes…

As the sun dawned and the alcohol and the arousal wore off, so did the truth dawn on Belinda. Lord Raven had not joined her, and she was glad. She felt sick at the thought of how that horrible man had so manipulated her human emotions as to turn her into a beast like himself. And she could see that working for him was only to be a matter of being a regularly beaten maid without the dessert of being the wife of a wealthy nobleman. Deciding this was not what she was seeking, and feeling bitterly remorseful at her behaviour the night before, she realised she must continue west as she slipped from the room and away from the estate before anyone else was awake enough to spot her.

Chapter Two

Belinda trudged all morning in a westward direction towards a vast mountain range. She was deeply upset by the previous night's promiscuous events, and she helped to keep her spirits up by singing *Greensleeves* and *Annie Laurie*, as well as humming and la-la-ing some of the brighter piano exercises she used to teach. She found the increasingly mountainous scenery breathtakingly beautiful, but deep depression returned as soon as she remembered the reality of her situation. To be destitute in a strange and hostile land was infinitely worse than being destitute back on the streets of Liverpool. She did not know how many miles still lay ahead of her, but she knew it was most of them. Perhaps she had been silly to slip away from Lord Raven's house without asking for some food or money for her journey, but she had been afraid that such a man might refuse to let her go. She started to cry as she dragged her feet through the dust. And worse, although she had eaten well the night before, her long walk had brought her appetite back with a will, and above all, she was very, very thirsty.

And then through her tears she saw a shimmering shape. Her heart skipped. It was a solitary but solid building at a junction in the road, and outside that building there was a stagecoach! Surely there would be some sort of help there, she thought as she started to hurry towards the stone erection.

Her spirits dropped as she observed that the stagecoach had no horses attached, but soared again when she saw that the driver was in a corral on the other side of the shack, in the process of changing steeds. And best of all, jolly male and female laughter and the smell of cooking were wafting out from the building, which was obviously some sort of inn.

She entered the gloomy room, a little unsure of herself. Although she still wore the thin low-cut gown that Lord Raven had given her, it was quite dusty and the hem was torn where she had snagged it on a thorn. Her hair and her face were also full of dust and she felt highly embarrassed by her appearance as she saw the well-dressed young group sitting at one of the three crude plank tables. They were chattering and shrieking with laughter, and hardly noticed Belinda at all.

But really it was that sophisticated-looking group which was out of place. The inn itself was coarsely constructed, dark, and not at all clean, with a faint odour of urine clinging to the air. Behind the bar, which consisted of two planks resting on a pair of barrels, stood a dumpy little man with a miserable face that was not enlivened by the fish-like eyes, which he shifted in Belinda's direction as she entered. He must have wondered how she had got there, but did not deign to ask as she approached.

'Good morning,' said Belinda hesitantly, but all she got in return was an almost imperceptible nod as the landlord continued to stare sullenly at her.

'I've had rather a bad time and an awfully long walk. Is there any chance of a glass of water, please?'

Belinda blushed with self-consciousness as the seated group fell silent on hearing her plea and her English accent.

'You want to buy a glass of water?' replied the landlord in a gritty voice as he surveyed her pure white cleavage and wondered what it would be like to put his hands up her dress.

'I'm afraid I haven't any money.' Belinda said

feebly. As regards his looking at her cleavage, she was simultaneously thinking that there was no way she would prostitute herself to that horrible man with his heavy unshaven jowls. She would find water somewhere else if necessary.

'This ain't no fucking charity, you whore,' snarled mein host, which made Belinda feel both suicidal and murderous all at the same time.

'Hey hey hey!' called out the thinner of the two men at the table. 'That's quite enough of that you filthy little curmudgeon!'

Belinda noticed his accent was American yet in a sort of English way, an observation that also applied to the group's well-cut style of dress.

'If you were to address a lady – any lady – in that way in Boston,' chipped in the darker of the two women in a plummy voice, 'you'd be tied to a lamppost, stripped naked and horse whipped.'

'Yeah, well, this ain't no Boston, thank God,' snarled the innkeeper.

'Oh, you're on speaking terms with God, are you?' piped up the other man, somewhat on the tubby side but with a jolly if hard air about him. 'Well, the old fellow's certainly gone downhill since the last time I went to church.'

This caused a lot of sniggering from his companions, and he too joined in the laughter. Belinda smiled as well. Then the thinner man spoke again.

'Give this poor girl a pint of your very best water and charge it to my bill as a pint of your filthy beer. And do it now.'

Satisfied with this, the owner shuffled into the back with a pint pot and returned moments later with it full of clean clear water. Belinda took it and, before quaffing from it, turned to the table and thanked the group.

'Not at all, my dear,' said the slim man in the most charming way.

'Perhaps she's hungry as well,' whispered the brunette loudly. So far her younger blonde friend had said nothing but sat smiling sweetly at everything that went on.

'Quite right, honey!' cried the thin gentleman. A pair of tears stung Belinda's eyes briefly. Bill, her dead husband-to-be, had called her 'honey', in the few words he'd had time to say to her. 'Please, will you join us? It would be an honour to have you.'

What delightful people these were, Belinda thought, as she sat beside the two women who had shuffled along the rough bench to make room for her. She sat down beside the young blonde, who did not seem to mind that their thighs were pressed together due to the limited space.

'Come along, you oaf!' shouted the tubby man to the owner. 'Bad news for your pigs, you're going to have to sell some more of their swill to a human being!'

The miserable landlord did not mind abuse as long as it was sales related, and he hurried out to the back again, returning in half a minute with a plateful of stew, which actually looked and smelt very appetising. He banged it down in front of Belinda along with a dirty spoon and went back to the bar, having taken an order for a fresh round of drinks for the group. The ladies both drank gin and water whilst the men preferred whisky and beer together. They also insisted on ordering a gin for Belinda, even though she was happy with the fresh well water.

The stagecoach driver came in with his guard, a pair of tough but honest looking men. The driver announced that the horses were changed and they'd be off in about half an hour, as soon as he and his partner had eaten.

While the deplorable coach station owner busied himself with the stagecoach crew, the group introduced themselves. The thin man was called Timothy and his fatter friend was Oliver, whilst the brunette went by the name of Marie and her blonde companion was called Jane. They were not married and they were, as Belinda had already heard, from Boston and were as wealthy as they were witty. They had become bored with polite Boston society and were on a slumming it adventure holiday, looking for whatever laughs might come their way.

'I guess you could say we're game for any old bit of excitement,' said Timothy to Belinda, looking down his nose at her with a wicked aristocratic smile, which she found rather electrifying.

'But pray, Belinda,' said Marie a little haughtily, 'if it's not too impertinent, what's an English girl doing out here in the wilderness without a penny or a horse? You are English, are you not?'

'Yes, I'm from Liverpool, actually,' said Belinda, taking a sip of her gin and water.

And she told them of how she had come out in search of a new life, without mentioning her old life, and how Bill had been slain within minutes of their meeting. She also told them about Lord Raven and how she had watched the slave Rosie being beaten, albeit more or less voluntarily. Again, she omitted her role in that ritual.

Blonde Jane, speaking for the first time, was most intrigued by the events at Lord Raven's plantation, and went over and over the details with Belinda. She clearly found the situation quite thrilling and her little pink tongue darted in and out, licking her lips below her eagerly shining eyes.

Chubby Oliver, with beer dribbling down his shiny badly shaven chin, wanted to know where she thought she was heading, since she seemed to be directing herself deeper into the wilderness. They were astonished enough to exchange sudden smirks when she said California, though none of them knew of a place called The Angels, in English or in Spanish.

After some debate, Timothy advised her through heavy eyelids that her best, indeed her only, hope was to head for St Joseph on the banks of the Missouri, which was the jumping off point for most of the wagon trains. She'd be sure to find a train or a family to let her work her passage, a phrase that made Marie and Jane suppress snorts of amusement.

'Oliver,' drawled Jane elegantly with a lopsided smirk, 'doesn't our stage pass by that new cattle railroad to St Joseph?'

'Why yes, it surely does, Jane,' the fat man replied through greasy lips. 'Passes within a couple of miles in fact, some time tomorrow morning.'

'Well there we are!' cried Marie, clapping her hands. 'We need entertainment and she needs a lift!'

'Ah ha!' said Timothy brightly. 'Yes! Belinda, you didn't seem too condemnatory of old Lord Raven's carry on last night. Perhaps if you joined in some rather modern games with us in the coach we'd be inclined to pay your passage to within walking distance of a train that'll take you to all them wagons in about two days. How about it?'

Belinda allowed a grin to slowly spread across her face as she looked at his handsome features. She also felt Jane's thigh press harder against her own.

'Yes, please,' she whispered demurely, looking

forward to a stagecoach ride in the right direction and many sessions of cards and I-Spy and the like. If the fun flagged she would entertain them with a selection of songs, both traditional and modern.

Oliver startled everyone by giving a whoop of joy at her response, and throwing himself backwards against his chair as he did so. Unfortunately he had forgotten they were sitting on benches, not chairs, and a look of shock crossed his face as he fell flat on his back on the floor.

His companions and Belinda looked worried for a moment until they saw he was unhurt. Then they all exploded into hysterical guffaws and shrieks of laughter. Oliver, still laying flat on his back, tried to glare at them but then he too had to burst out laughing...

The stage thundered along through the lower passes of the Appalachians, a most uncomfortable mode of travel. At first the group was sleepy from the heavy lunchtime drinking and they mainly dozed for the first couple of hours. Then, realising they were wasting precious Belinda-time, they had tried to play strip poker, a game Belinda had never heard of but had agreed to try to learn, but the cards kept bouncing all over the place and off the makeshift table they had made out of a leather valise balanced on their knees.

'Somebody ought to invent playing cards that can be used under these adverse conditions,' observed Marie as she passed the gin bottle to Belinda.

'Should be quite easy really,' sniffed Oliver. 'They just have to put thin magnets on the backs of each card and you use a metal plate to play on. Simple.'

'You are a cretin, Ollie!' laughed Timothy, flicking whisky into his friend's face. 'Magnets on the back?

31

All the cards would stick together, you'd never be able to deal them or fan them or…'

'I'm getting sexy,' interrupted Jane, looking at Belinda as she took the gin bottle from her. Belinda blinked with surprise at that, but her clitoris twitched involuntarily, causing her to blush at her own reaction. 'Can't we have the strip without bothering about the poker?' continued Jane. 'It's just nicely squashed in here. We could take it in turns to stand up and let the others have a good feel. Me first!'

And up jumped blonde Jane, standing in the tight space between the facing seats. The two men were on one side, and Marie and Belinda were on the other.

'Oh, I don't know, Jane,' sighed Marie. 'We've got each other forever, but we've only got Belinda for a couple of days. I say she stands up first.'

'Oh yes, why not?' said Jane pleasantly, and sat down again.

Belinda had been following the last few remarks with some astonishment and trepidation.

'I'll be master of ceremonies,' announced Oliver, and when nobody objected he continued, 'First of all, for greater comfort for us as well as heightened pleasure for the ladies, all gentlemen herein assembled are to get their cocks out.'

And the two Boston women watched excitedly as first Timothy and then Oliver undid their large fly buttons and opened their trousers wide. Belinda was too taken aback and embarrassed to say or do anything except stare as Tim and Oliver, after much rummaging around, produced two powerful penises. They were both very big but Timothy's was pale and circumcised whilst Oliver's was dark and quite thick in diameter.

The women watched as each man masturbated slowly for a few seconds, and then Oliver continued,

'Marie and Jane, you are both so sexy that my cock wants to see every bit of you right now. Slip off those dresses please or I'll throw you to the driver.'

Belinda, by now reluctant to tear her eyes from those handsome and wealthy pricks, nonetheless turned around to watch Jane and Marie. There was no room for them both to stand up, so they took it in turns to hoist their long dresses to their waists, kneel up on the hard bench seat and pull the gowns off over their heads. Both women had beautiful figures and, Belinda was pleased to note, like her they wore nothing underneath. She was now quite content with the turn of events, as she saw no harm in watching the behaviour of these strange Americans, especially as they didn't involve her. She could easily convince herself – and often did – that it was only wrong if you actually did something with someone else. But watching and, in private, masturbating, were entirely different matters.

Marie and Jane now sat naked on the narrow seat. Marie's nipples were strong and dark brown, which contrasted nicely with Jane's which were soft and bright pink. Marie fondled her own breasts as she looked at Belinda while Jane licked a middle finger, slipped it inside herself and made little moaning noises. Belinda watched with a small smile, as that of an old lady tolerating some high-spirited but harmless urchins. She was trying to ignore the tingling that was developing in the region at the top of her thighs.

'Excellent, ladies!' cried Oliver. 'Keep our guest entertained while Tim and I explore her hinterland. Stand up girl!' he added sharply to Belinda, whose face drained of colour.

'I'm sorry?' she asked coolly.

'On your feet, woman!' he repeated with some annoyance, his face turning almost as purple as the tip of his cock.

'I don't think you quite understand,' retorted Belinda. 'I don't mind what you all do for fun, but I'm not inclined to join in. I did, after all, come to America in search of a new start in life.'

'So you used to do this sort of thing back in merry old England, then?' Tim put in quickly and perceptively.

'Ah ha!' cried Oliver with a fat grin. 'What d'you say to that, then?'

'I'm sorry, I don't have to say anything,' stammered Belinda, blushing violently and briskly removing Jane's hand from her leg.

'I think we'd better get the driver to stop,' snarled Marie. 'English women obviously don't know the meaning of the word gratitude. If she can't stand a little bit of fun in return for a ride and a meal and lodging then it's best she gets out and walks.'

'Hear bloody hear!' jeered Oliver whilst Tim and Jane made similar noises of agreement.

Belinda was horrified at the thought of being dumped in the passing wilderness. She hesitated.

'Oh, come on old girl,' wheedled Tim. 'Just as far as the next coach house. You can stay overnight and tomorrow you can do what you like. How's that sound?'

Belinda considered. She sighed. She nodded. She had little choice. She stood up and faced the ladies, to raucous cheers and whoops from her new friends.

Jane and Marie played their part with gusto. Each one leant back as much as possible and gazed into Belinda's face whilst playing with their breasts and stroking their thighs with extravagant movements.

Belinda gasped with surprise as she felt a hand at each of her ankles. Glancing quickly behind she saw

34

that Tim was starting to tickle her legs. Her knees banged involuntarily together at the sensation of the two hands stroking their way up towards her thighs. Standing inside the lurching stagecoach, looking down on two beautiful girls masturbating whilst a handsome man's hands stroked their way up her inner thigh, it was not surprising that Belinda should secretly feel, for the first time in a couple of years, that she was approaching heaven. Her morals had been suspended due to the overwhelming nature of her plight and circumstances, and when Timothy finally grasped her vagina from behind, pressing the flat of his hand hard against it whilst his middle finger drummed against her jumping clitoris, she knew she was truly in paradise. She moaned and abandoned all her mental resistance.

By the time Jane and then Marie had also enjoyed a turn at putting their hands up Belinda's dress to fondle and tickle her concealed sex she was almost delirious with desire.

'Oh my god! Oh my god!' she heard Timothy groan, and when she turned around she saw he was masturbating faster and faster, his lust having taken control of his willpower. With the speed of an experienced member of an emergency service, Oliver whipped out a large white linen handkerchief and spread it over Timothy's shirt to protect it, and Belinda, inflamed, turned to face Timothy and pulled her dress up to her waist exposing herself fully for the first time since she had met this group. Her lovely triangle of dark hair glistened deliciously and the burning sensation all around it increased as Timothy groaned intensely. The speed of his fist accelerated furiously and in a few seconds he roared, arched his back and shot powerfully. His pure white seed spat into the air. Some landed on the thoughtfully positioned kerchief, whilst even more splattered into Belinda's cleavage and in her hair. At the same moment she spun around to see Jane and Marie bring themselves to simultaneous orgasms.

The two ladies slumped in their seats. Tim's penis throbbed slowly downwards, stopping at half mast. Only Oliver's powerful piece remained ready to give Belinda that which she was in little condition to resist. He smiled up at her as he fingered himself. 'I do hope you don't mind, dear girl,' he smiled, 'but it's now time to give you a good hard shagging.'

'I, um, don't really want to go that far...' she stammered in alarm.

'And you ain't going to get very far with that attitude neither,' sneered Oliver. 'You'd rather get out and walk?'

On the obese side though he was, there was nothing intrinsically wrong with Oliver's looks, and certainly nothing wrong with his long broad prick. And anyway, the overwhelming sexual lust that had temporarily taken control of Belinda's body and soul would have made even that awful innkeeper acceptable at this point in time. She sighed inwardly; she told her conscience she had tried to be good but everything was stacked against her and she begged forgiveness. She nodded as Oliver started to stand.

'And I want you from behind,' he whispered wickedly.

Belinda no longer cared as long as he got it over with, but there were practical considerations to be borne in mind.

'But there's no room...' she breathed, unable to complete the sentence.

But Oliver was on his feet, balancing himself against the swaying carriage wherever he could get a grip. He took hold of Belinda and roughly manoeuvred her to face the door. Then he bent her forward so her top half went out through the open window and was exposed to the rushing air, the dust, the grit, the noise and the dizzy sensation of the ground dashing past at close quarters.

She felt her dress being raised again at the back and then a lovely warm feeling as his cock lay in the valley of her pillowy white bottom. The driver glanced backwards and down as she caught his eye, and she had enough self-possession to find it gratifying that he did not know what was going on inside.

He looked forward again and cracked the whip over the horses. This triggered a conditioned response in Belinda, and her already wet vagina felt like it was flooding. There was a sharp pressure from behind and Oliver's enormous tool shot between her legs and into her. Once inside he moved back and forth viciously, the powerfully sized prick filling her more than she could remember ever having been filled by that groom. And the overwhelmingly beautiful sensation in her clitoris as the head of that superb cock slid up and down contrasted deliciously with the crippling pain across her stomach where Oliver's weight pressed her down against the window frame of the door as the world flew by oblivious to what Belinda was experiencing.

She felt the orgasm growing within and Ollie pumped harder in perfect rhythm with the increasing intensity of the feeling. God that fat man could fuck! And as she started to come she felt that he too was starting his climax and she closed her eyes tight against the stinging dust.

A strange and wonderful feeling went through her as her orgasm – and his – shuddered through her body.

She suddenly felt as if she were flying free through the air, yet the sense of weightlessness was counteracted in the weirdest way by an agonising increase in the weight of Ollie pressing her against the wood. Perturbed, she opened her eyes and was aghast to find that the stagecoach door had swung open under their pressure and was swinging freely with the two of them leaning across it. She just had time to scream her terror before they both plummeted headfirst to almost certain death on the rushing ground below...

It was fortunate for their lives, if not their dignity, that the stagecoach had at that moment drawn up outside the staging post where they were to spend the night.

The two of them fell to the stony ground in a bundled heap, Oliver with his trousers down and Belinda with her bare bottom up. As they realised they were unhurt they blinked and almost died of embarrassment instead of impact. A miserable looking woman and her two equally ungracious children stared down at them – and their exposed parts – in disgust. The driver's and the guard's screeches of laughter did nothing to help, nor did the applause, cheers and cries of 'Encore!' from Timothy, Marie and Jane as they peered out from the coach.

But the woman started to scream abusively and, grabbing a cane from where it was leaning against the building, rushed at the two prone figures and started lashing at their naked rumps, shouting frenzied insults. She was not joking and they both found the shock of the lash severely agonising until the stagecoach crew and Oliver's friends dragged the hag off – but only after they had enjoyed the spectacle for a few minutes.

As they picked themselves up, Oliver glared at Belinda and said calmly, 'You won't find that in the

Kama Sutra, but it's the way we always do things in Boston.'

After dinner they found the presence of the old virago who ran the station so oppressive that they bought some bottles of spirits from her and wandered well away from the buildings to start a camp fire and have some fun of their own.

The woman's foul disposition made the previous innkeeper seem as happy as a clown who had just inherited a circus. Her unpleasantness was far more positive than his had been. She had continually criticised the group throughout their meal, and when they bought a drink she demanded to know why people needed such things as alcohol, and didn't they know it would poison their souls as well as their bodies. When Oliver asked how come she sold the stuff she went berserk, which was when they beat their retreat to the safety of the savage land around them.

In spite of her bruising from the fall, Belinda felt more at peace than she had for many a month. The moon was the biggest she had ever seen and the camp fire kept the chill of the night away. They were seated by a tiny copse. One trunk was lying on the ground beside its stump, which helped to create the illusion that they were in their own private enclosure. She didn't begrudge her companions their bit of fun with her that afternoon in the stagecoach, but she had decided that she wanted no more of that sort of thing and would walk or seek alternative transport the next day.

The gin she had been drinking all afternoon, and which she was drinking now, also contributed warmly to her feeling of relaxation and wellbeing, and after a while, in response to probing questions about her life in England, she opened up and told them all about her tribulations.

They seemed very sad to hear about her father and brother, and did not condemn them in any way. But they were more than interested to hear of how she had scraped a living on the streets of Liverpool. They all found her accounts very exciting, and Jane in particular wanted Belinda to go over the best bits in great detail. Her audience's great interest in her tales was clearly illustrated by the way the dancing firelight showed up their wide shining eyes.

'Heavens,' breathed Timothy. 'You mean there are actually people who get sexually aroused by administering corporal punishment to girls?'

'Well,' said Marie, 'I can quite understand that, Tim. I'm getting aroused just hearing about it.'

'Oh God, so am I!' cried Jane in a fierce whisper.

'Well, if you must know,' chipped in Oliver, a look of sleepy drunkenness on his shiny unshaven face, 'I had it done to me once.'

Everyone, including Belinda, looked at him in surprise; not shock, they were all too sophisticated for that.

'You mean you did it to a girl once, surely?' said a puzzled Timothy.

'No, not at all,' continued Oliver with a smug smirk. 'A certain society hostess whom we all know, a few years older than I, made me the offer. She invited me for a walk in her grounds one night. Then she took hold of my cock and "Ollie" she said, "you've got a great big penis and a great big backside". She was gently pulling me through my thin pants as she spoke, and then she made me the offer: I could have all the sex I wanted with her as long as she could strap, smack, and cane my bottom as much as she wanted.

40

Well, I definitely favoured her – you'd agree if I broke my word and told you who it was – and I thought she wouldn't have the strength to make any serious impression on my derriere. But heavens, she had a strong right arm! I had to let her tie me down in the end else I couldn't have stood there and took it.'

Jane's eyes flashed. 'And did you enjoy it?' she asked intensely.

'It was awful!' shrieked Ollie. 'But then afterwards, every time I thought about it I got a rock hard-on. In the end I went back to her for more. And got it!'

There was a long pause after he finished, broken only by eerie bird cries in the distance.

'All this debauched talk is making my heart thump quite alarmingly,' Jane eventually broke the silence prettily. 'Tell me Belinda, did you find it exciting or was it terrifying?'

'Well,' said Belinda, quite enjoying being the expert, 'at first I just couldn't believe the flaming pain. But then it got just like Oliver said; whenever I thought about it I became so overwhelmed by the sensational fire in my clit...' her voice faded quickly as she realised what she was admitting. 'You just get used to it...' she concluded hurriedly.

There was an even longer silence as the group digested what they had been hearing. At last Timothy spoke.

'Well, judging by the look on Jane's face, not to mention Marie's and Oliver's, I'd guess we'd all be in favour of trying some of this out ourselves. I personally, ladies and gentleman, have got a hard-on that could be used to break the ice in the Hudson River.'

'Yeah,' added Oliver, now fully awake, 'mine wouldn't have to break the ice, it's goddam hot enough to melt it!'

Marie laughed delightedly and clapped her hands. 'Oh golly, I'm so excited I don't know what to do or where to start!'

'What shall we do, Belinda?' asked Jane, snuggling closer to Belinda and caressing one of her soft breasts through the thin cotton gown. 'You know all about it.'

Exciting as Belinda found Jane's touch, she moved away firmly. 'No, I'm sorry,' she said. 'I agreed to do what we did in the coach but that's it. No more.'

'But you're going to need a lift tomorrow as well if you want to catch a wagon train to the West,' gloated Marie huskily.

'No, I've thought about that and I'll just have to manage one way or another. After all, I am a music teacher from a good family. There are more important things to a lady of my standing than what might or might not happen tomorrow.'

'Oh come on, Belinda, for God's sake!' cried Tim impatiently.

'No,' she replied firmly.

They all glared at her.

'I don't see why you want to make such a nightmare journey to California,' said Jane gently, 'when you aren't even sure of what awaits you there. Poor Belinda; why don't you come back to Boston with us? We would find you decent employment to begin with, wouldn't't we Timmy?'

An excited smile flooded Timothy's face. 'Well of course we would, if she showed herself to be a true friend,' he said, staring at Belinda in a way that made her tremble all over.

'And then after a while,' chirped Jane, 'why, you could save up and start earning your own living giving music lessons again. Boston is a very cultured city and there's a big demand for music teachers.'

The four Bostonians watched Belinda carefully for her reaction. She was clearly impressed with this suggestion.

'And I'm sure a woman of your charm and intelligence would be running her own Academy of the Musical Arts within a year. Especially with our backing,' said Oliver in a very persuasive tone; not at all nice – just persuasive.

'Yes, but would that mean I'd have to be dirty with you all the way up to Boston?' Belinda said at last. 'It must be a week or more to get there.'

This was met with an immediate chorus of 'no' and 'of course not', and it was Jane who added, 'Just give us one wildly fanciful night tonight, and we'll leave you alone all the rest of the way.'

She smiled longingly in a way that excited Belinda and made her worry, not for the first time, about the way she always found herself easily stirred by a good-looking girl. But she had little time to brood on the realization at that point in time. The unaccustomed day of gin drinking was making her bolder than she would normally have been, and the offer of a bright and cultured future in a civilised city seemed to be a goal she would certainly sacrifice one more night for. After all, necessity had driven her into strange and unwelcome situations many times already in her life. And she didn't think this little group posed any real threat to her as regards inflicting pain. 'Well... all right then,' she said cautiously.

There were cheers from her companions, not without a hint of gloating.

'What shall we do then?' asked Marie breathlessly. 'You're the expert.'

Belinda felt a flush of deep shame and

embarrassment at that remark, but she had to admit that Marie was right. Compared to these innocent fun lovers she was, alas, the one with all the experience. She blinked back the tears that were forming and rallied her spirits.

'I think it's best if we make a game of it. I think Timothy should be the one who does it to start off, he's definitely the type, but what shall the game be?' She looked at the others expectantly, awaiting suggestions. But they were all staring at her. She thought a moment, and then brightened.

'I know,' she said with a happy smile. 'Timothy's a dead strict gentleman and we're his household servants. And he's not too happy with our work so he says he's to punish us. And we have to put up with it because he pays double the wages of anyone else, and anyhow there's no other jobs going either. That's a very popular one back home.'

Timothy beamed his appreciation of the idea, whilst the two girls and Oliver made lots of excited noises about it.

'And I suggest you have to send one of us back to get that old woman's cane from outside the inn. Right?' Belinda's future was at stake here and she was not going to risk spoiling her chances by holding herself back.

'Right!' grinned Timothy.

'Well, go on then!' Belinda had to prompt him, and at that he jumped up as quickly as his slightly inebriated state would allow and faded into the shadows. They were just beginning to wonder where he had gone when he made them all jump by suddenly striding into the makeshift camp from behind them, saying angrily, 'Right, all household staff stand up!'

They quickly got to their feet, Jane first and Oliver

last, and Timothy stood there surveying them with realistic contempt.

'Right you inferior scum, it's Friday. That means it's pay day and, as you know, before I pay you your wages I have to consider how to pay you for everything you have failed to complete to my satisfaction since last week.'

He studied them haughtily. He was playing his role so well that Belinda felt the skin of her bottom tingling and tensing.

'And I have to tell you,' continued Timothy, 'that I am not a jot happy with any of you this week. Jane, go and fetch my cane at once.'

'Not the cane, master!' cried Belinda for effect.

But Jane was already gone, running as fast as her long dress would allow.

'How dare you interrupt me, Belinda!' thundered Timothy. 'Come here!'

Belinda hurried to stand in front of him. Staring into her eyes, he moved his hand forward and pressed it against her soft vulva, holding it there for a few seconds and then rubbing gently but firmly up and down. Both he and she found her thin cotton dress added to the smoothness without blunting any of the sensation, and she pressed herself hard against his hand. After a minute he removed it, placed both arms around her waist and pulled her tight to him so that his penis, bold and hard, was rubbing up and down her slit. His hands slid up her back, and then one of them moved around to the front to gently squeeze her nearest nipple. With a couple of deft movements he had expertly flopped her right breast out through the plunging neckline, and was caressing it in the cool night air when Jane came hurrying back into the camp circle. She approached Timothy holding the cane out towards him with great reverence.

Timothy released Belinda. She stepped back, leaving her fleshy white breast exposed, the pinkness of its nipple enhanced by the firelight.

Timothy tested the cane by swishing it through the air a few times. Belinda noticed Jane's tongue dart across her dry lips as she watched this display with sparkling eyes. She realised at that moment that although she was predominantly inclined towards men in matters of romance, she would rather have a sexual encounter with Jane than with any of the others.

'Jane!' called Timothy sharply and beckoned her to follow him. He went and stood by the tree stump and unbuttoned his trousers. He pulled his penis out and solemnly showed it to the ladies and Oliver. He then ordered Jane to remove his trousers, which she did, taking care to lick the tip of his stalk as she bent down.

'Jane, you're a very naughty maidservant, but you're not the worst. I'm going to let you off with a spanking across my knee, and then you can help me deal with the rest of this idle bunch of layabouts.'

Her tongue was still toying with his glistening tip, and he took hold of her silvery-blonde hair and pulled her head firmly into his groin as he smiled pompously at the others. Marie and Oliver were watching with bright-eyed anticipation, and Belinda was very impressed by Timothy's act. He certainly caught on quickly for someone who had never played this sort of game before. She found herself envying Jane for having Tim's potent piece in her mouth, and at the same time she envied Tim for having Jane's intimate attention. She felt powerfully attracted to that pretty young lady.

Timothy pushed Jane's head away, and the wet point of his penis shone brightly in the flickering light.

Belinda felt her body being overtaken by lust as she recalled how he had masturbated in the coach earlier that day. And now he sat on the tree stump with his cock pounding dramatically as it stood up from his lap. He kicked his trousers away from his ankles, gripped Jane by the wrist and pulled her towards him, causing her to utter a cry that was a mixture of alarm and excitement.

'Right my girl!' he cried. 'Get that dress up high please!'

Jane obeyed immediately, pulling her full dress up to her waist, and Belinda and the other two saw her beautiful satiny white bottom fully displayed towards them. Her vagina was close to Timothy, and they saw him lean forward slightly and kiss her fluffy blonde pubic hairs briefly. He then pulled her down across his bare lap and settled her into position, which included grabbing her nearest hand and making her hold his prick as best as she could. Her face was close to the ground and she looked very serious as she keenly awaited this new sensation.

As Timothy started to squeeze and explore Jane's bottom and thighs, Belinda felt a pair of lips brush her ear. Marie had slipped behind her and whispered softly, 'This is fantastic. I'm so glad we met you. I feel so worked up. Do you mind?' And before Belinda could ask did she mind what, she felt Marie's bosom press hard against her back and her arms encircle her waist from behind. The brunette's hands tickled Belinda's stomach, and then gradually worked their way down to where they could feel the start of her hair through the thin cotton dress.

'You are a bad girl,' Timothy said quietly and raised his hand high, paused, and then slapped down hard on Jane's soft sweet buttock. She jumped, squealed, and

47

wriggled as her face and bottom flushed red together. But she stayed in position while Timothy repeated the ritual of fondling, squeezing, pausing and then slapping her white backside.

Marie, still holding Belinda, whispered again, 'Look, oh look at the way the head of his cock goes purple every time she squeezes it after each smack!' and she added to the sexual charge that this statement had injected into Belinda by dropping her right hand to the English girl's clitoris and pressing it ferociously with the tip of her middle finger. At the same time her left hand raced up Belinda's stomach and found the exposed breast. Belinda, thoroughly enjoying this attention in spite of herself, slipped her hands behind and prodded her fingertips against Marie's succulent mound of pleasure.

The two women masturbated each other with increasing passion as Timothy made Jane stand up and started to tweak and slap her thighs. He worked slowly and methodically, pausing only now and again to give his penis a few slow pulls as he studied the squirming Marie and Belinda as well as Jane. Oliver was watching intently too and was rubbing his bulging trouser front quite vigorously.

As Timothy turned Jane to face the others, with her back to him so he could spank the backs of her thighs he gasped, 'I'm not going to be able to do all of you. I'm going to go all the way with Jane's bottom and then I'm going to roger her over that tree trunk! This really is superb fun, it really is.'

Jane, standing with her dress held high and her eyes closed in ecstasy, whimpered as he spoke, a sound that was echoed in Belinda's ear as Marie breathed, 'Oh God, Belinda, then let me do you – please, please, please!'

48

That alone was almost enough to make the hitherto reluctant Belinda come, and she nodded her vigorous agreement as they turned to face each other and embraced passionately, their nipples pressed deliciously together. Their fervent hug was interrupted by three sharp cracks, and they looked around to see that Timothy had bent Jane over the fallen tree trunk and had already started to cane the backs of her thighs. On the third ringing report Jane screamed, 'That's it! No more!' whereupon Timothy, his cock bouncing in front of him, gave her one last swipe with the whippy stick, catching her expertly in the crease between her buttocks and her legs. She screamed again and spun around as Timothy threw the cane down and hurried forward. He lifted the small blonde onto the tree trunk in a sitting position and moved in between her legs, at the same time taking hold of his penis and aiming it towards the delicious patch of fur at the top of her thighs.

As Belinda and Marie watched, Belinda felt her dress rise at the back and something hot and hard press against the valley of her bottom. She sighed resignedly and urged back against Oliver's ample cock, feeling it against her behind for the second time that day. Keeping his tip hard against her anus he helped Marie strip her of her dress. Belinda peered over her shoulder and saw he was naked, his large figure quite in proportion with his hefty organ. She fumbled and gave it a rub of appreciation. As she did so she felt something long thin and cold slide between her legs. It was the cane. Marie had picked it up and was now using it in a sawing motion to tickle Belinda's crease and Oliver's scrotum.

'Caught you,' Marie whispered wickedly. 'Now I'm going to have to punish you, aren't I?'

49

She withdrew the cane from between their legs, giving Belinda's right buttock a vicious and very prolonged pinch as she did so. Belinda marvelled at how thoroughly the group had thrown themselves into this sort of activity, and was glad she had had enough experience in England to enable her to pretend to enjoy it with these friendly if somewhat immoral people.

She jumped out of this absentminded thinking as she felt a sting on the front of her leg. Marie had flicked her with the stick.

'Get over that tree trunk beside those other two fornicators!' she snarled, very realistically, and Belinda and Ollie shuffled over as ordered. Belinda bent beside Timothy and Jane who were screwing slowly. Jane's legs and arms were wrapped tightly around Timothy to stop herself from falling off the trunk. They both watched as best they could as Marie started to calmly and scientifically cane Belinda and Oliver. The only sign that this was a sexual experience for Marie was to be observed in the way she kept her free hand pressed against her prominent vagina as it lay deeply hidden in her dark bush.

Oliver shrieked so horribly at each resounding crack that Belinda was sure he would have to ask to be tied down, but he maintained his position until Marie had finished. Belinda herself found Marie's strokes across her bottom and legs to be very stimulating, and she did not have to simulate any agonised sounds; Marie was vicious and as she progressed with the beating Belinda screamed as loudly as Oliver. She did, however, have the small comfort of a bump on the tree trunk that pressed hard against her slit, and each stroke of the stick served to press her hard against it.

By the time Marie stopped both Oliver's and Belinda's rumps were ablaze. She might well have carried on all night had not Timothy, now finished with Jane, taken the cane and bent her over so as to give her some of the same.

'Hold me!' she shouted as she was pushed over the rough wood, and Oliver happily obliged by nipping around to the other side and gripping her wrists tightly. As Timothy slashed the cane at Marie with the frenzy of the newly converted, Jane took Belinda by the breasts and pressed her to the ground. She climbed on top of her and their legs intertwined. They worked their thighs hard against each other's vagina and mauled each other's breasts while the sound of the cane rained deservedly down on Marie's naked backside, with the stick and Timothy's rising and falling arm silhouetted against the enormous moon.

They were all tired and sore as the stagecoach bounced along the next morning, but none of the young Bostonians had any regrets about the evening's entertainment, and such enthusiasm as they could muster was used to praise Belinda, to her great embarrassment, for the education she had given them. However, that was all behind her now and she had an exciting future awaiting in Boston. She felt she could now look forward to a life free of sexual taint, until the right man took her for his wife.

'I can't wait to get to Boston and start working in a decent job,' she said with her girlish excitement, but was concerned to find that they replied with less enthusiasm. In fact it was received with a certain uneasiness.

'Yes... that might, ah, prove a little awkward,' said Oliver without looking at her.

Belinda felt a sickening lurch in her stomach.

'We were talking it over last night...' continued

51

Oliver, and then he hesitated.

'You see, Boston is a funny sort of town,' said Timothy. 'Everyone has their place in the social order.'

Belinda's biggest shock came from Marie. 'You're just not our class, darling. You'd never be allowed to mix with us you know.' And she said it as if she fully supported that system!

'You wouldn't like it,' chipped in Jane with a hint of sympathy. 'You'd only be able to work in a very low position.'

'Like letting people whack your arse for money,' sniffed Oliver sarcastically and somewhat hypocritically.

'It just wouldn't work,' added Timothy, his hands giving a wide-open gesture of 'hard luck but that's life'.

The tears that sprung into Belinda's eyes at this genuinely heartless and shallowly snobbish rejection prevented her from speaking further, but a minute later she was saved from further embarrassment by the stagecoach slowing down and the driver shouting, 'St Joseph's railroad!'

As Belinda wandered away from the coach in a daze she was further mortified to hear beautiful friendly little Jane saying to the others, 'Goodness; just imagine us going back home with that in tow!'

Chapter Three

Exhausted, heartbroken and in a state of great moral confusion as she was, Belinda's spirits initially soared when she arrived at St Joseph in Missouri, on the border with Kentucky. For there on the banks of the mighty river that gave the state its name, were gathered a dozen giant steamships and covered wagons galore amidst such a scene of lively commotion far in excess of anything she had ever beheld in the Liverpool docks.

It was three days after she had left the stagecoach and had climbed onto the empty cattle train as it slowed for a sharp curve close to where her former 'friends' had dropped her off. It had been a miserable journey due to the lack of food and only the occasional chance to grab a drink of water by jumping off and back on each time the train started to move away from its watering points. And when the locomotive finally came to a shuddering screeching halt north of the tiny township called Kansas City she still had a whole night's weary walk to undergo before she reached St Joseph.

She mingled with the crowds, the swirling dust and smell of human and horse flesh almost suffocating, but the overwhelming impression was in the way the atmosphere was electrified by the constant cracking of whips; whips being cracked in the air out of high spirits or as demonstrations of skill. Whips were cracking over the backs of horses and oxen. A gigantic black man was being whipped on his back at one place, whilst further on Belinda passed a bare-breasted adolescent blonde who was also being lashed on her back by a man who might have been her father. In each of the latter cases an amused crowd stood around watching and cheering.

Belinda wondered if she had died and woken up in hell as she plodded on, looking out for a family or group that might help her. But they were all incredibly rude. Some just swore and shoved her away roughly, whilst others were very coarse, loudly offering to take her on if she sucked them all the way to California, and then laughing uproariously. Belinda decided she would save those sort of options for last; there must surely be some decent people going west who would employ her as a servant on the journey.

And then, after trudging around the mighty gathering of covered wagons all morning and half the afternoon, she saw a sight that gave her wretched soul an uplift. A very religious-looking group with four wagons, each apparently owned by stern faced men with beards and their equally solemn wives. They were all dressed simply in black. There were no children to be seen, except for a teenage boy on one wagon and a girl of similar age on another, and the group looked ready to be on the move. They were scanning the crowds, as if there was something they were seeking before they left. Belinda, with nothing to lose, but also without any hope in her heart, approached the nearest man of the group.

'Excuse me, sir...' she said hesitantly, and trembled as he looked down fiercely from the wagon. The combination of her weariness, the abysmal behaviour of those Bostonians, and the thought of the enormous journey ahead had sapped her confidence.

'I... I'm English and I'm stranded and I have got to get to California.'

The man looked at her coldly. 'We are Danish and

54

we are stranded and we have to get to California too. We are of the very strict Pandervest religion, and we do not permit any work on the Sabbath. This can be arranged when you are at home, but on a long arduous and perilous journey such as this there will be things to do every day. We had arranged for a good girl to help us but she has not arrived and we can only see blackguards all around us looking for work.' He stared at her. He was a handsome man in a severe sort of way. 'But now I see the Lord has sent us an honest looking girl who is desperate too. Does that mean you wish to travel with us as our servant – especially on the Sabbath?'

Belinda could hardly believe her luck. Her eyes shone and her head nodded enthusiastically.

'Very well,' he continued, 'but we are a devout group and we have certain conditions for outsiders who are bound to break the Sabbath. I had better tell you them all…'

But Belinda didn't care. She was on her way to her uncle in California under the protection of a decent civilised group of families, and that was all that mattered.

'You can teach me as we journey!' she cried out. 'Whatever it is will be fine with me!'

'When can you leave?' asked the man, and he almost smiled when Belinda shouted, 'Now if you like!'

'If the good Lord likes, then now it will be,' he said in a wise tone of voice. He indicated to her to climb aboard, and his unsmiling wife, seated beside him, helped her up as he turned and called out the news in Danish to his companions. They restricted themselves to a few grunts of approval and, with Belinda safely aboard with those strange but decent folk, the four wagons moved down to the waterside to board the next ferry. They were to make the river crossing that afternoon, and then set off in earnest at daybreak the next day – Tuesday.

The first few days passed uneventfully; just a matter of trundling along all day, making as much progress as possible through the beautiful green and woody countryside and making camp at night. Belinda now felt that hell was far behind her and that everything would be all right from now on. She had been feeling that there must have been some innate wickedness in her soul that somehow showed through and made so many men want to defile her; she could think of no other reason for the strange reactions she inspired, both in Liverpool and in America. Perhaps it was some divine punishment for her family's crime. But here on the trail she was treated as one of the group, and the others shared the chores with her equally. She had no sensation of being a servant and developed a certain affection for the strange sect. There were, however, two incidents that livened up the monotony of the early days of that ever-westward journey.

Due to lack of space Belinda had to sleep in the open, though she was well provided with enough blankets to make this a pleasure rather than a penance. But on the Thursday, just as dusk had eaten away the last of the daylight, there was a sudden cloudburst and everyone scrambled for their wagons. Anna, the wife of Thonnig, the man who had given her the job, shouted at Belinda to get in with them quickly, and Belinda scurried to jump aboard and throw herself into the tiny space which was already full with the prone bodies of the two adults as well as the teenage boy of the group, their son Jens. He too usually slept outside but had leapt in ahead of the others when the storm broke. It was pitch black in the tiny wagon, and Belinda had no idea which body was which as she squeezed uncomfortably between them.

In spite of the discomfort, they all soon fell asleep as the rain lashed outside and the wind whipped through the canvas of the wagon. But in the middle of the night Belinda woke with a start to feel a hand gripping her leg just above the knee. She knew it was no accident because the hand was under her long skirt, and as she lay there hardly breathing, the hand moved further up her thighs. She had no idea whether it was the father or the son, but she dared not move or cry out for fear of causing trouble. She would have simply removed the hand from her leg but her arms were trapped by the press of bodies, and to move them would have caused a disturbance. Her experience of life so far told her that whatever happened she would be the one who was blamed.

Having made that decision, she further decided that she had no choice but to lie back until this horrible little incident was over, and still pretending to be asleep, she found herself unwittingly luxuriating in the tickling sensation as the roughened fingertips stroked their way higher and higher. Her breathing became difficult to control as those illicit fingers brushed the lips of her sensual vulva, and she once again desperately tried to work out which of them was doing it, though without success. She gave up and settled back for what had now become a lovely secret fondling when she gave a sudden sharp gasp. The intruding fingers, after first exploring inside her moist pit, now gripped those sensitive lips and pinched them, quite hard at first but then with increasing viciousness until it was all she could do to stop herself crying out. The fingers were so strong that she felt her vagina was being crushed by a pair of pliers, and she wanted nothing more than to relieve the agony by screaming loudly. Her secret tormentor relaxed the vicious grip for a few moments to play with her clitoris and explore inside, but just as Belinda was beginning once more to relax and savour the sensations the hand suddenly grabbed her entire vulva and twisted it savagely. Belinda could stand no more and was just about to shriek out her agony when the hand suddenly released its grip and slid gently back down to just above her knee. Once there it gave one firm pinch and then disappeared.

Belinda spent most of the next day carefully studying Thonnig and Jens for a clue as to which one it had been, but eventually gave up the exercise as futile. It did amuse her to think that at least one of this dedicated religious group had done such a thing, but then she recalled that some of the gentlemen in England who used to pay her to be beaten had been men of the cloth.

On the very next evening the tranquil life on the trail was disturbed yet again. The four wagons were in their usual square formation, there being too few to form a circle. Thonnig and his son Jens were chopping more wood for the fire whilst Belinda, Anna and the teenage girl Helle were clearing up after the evening meal, all working with quiet solemnity.

Suddenly Thonnig spoke sharply to his son in Danish and the boy replied in a tone that clearly carried a note of insolence. A shocked silence fell over the little camp as Jens and his father glared at each other. Thonnig said something quietly to Anna, and she left her chores and went to their wagon. Belinda

58

felt chilled when she saw Anna return moments later carrying a long cane with a walking stick handle. It was obvious what was about to happen and Belinda felt upset because Jens was a nice boy, the only cheerful one in the whole group. If she had thought it would have done any good she would have offered to have taken the caning for him, but knew there was little point in interfering.

Thonnig took the slender stick from his wife and led the boy out of the camp to a tree, followed by the rest of the group, including the pretty blonde Helle. Her marble complexion was flushed and her blossoming bosom swelled. She seemed as distressed as Belinda was, but the rest of the group were as solemn and wooden as ever. Belinda took up a position at the back and to one side of the group.

The exact form of the ritual that followed took Belinda by some surprise, given that it was such a religious sect. Thonnig stood Jens with his back to the tree facing the group, which sat down to watch the spectacle. All except Petta, one of the wives, whom Thonnig called forward. She knelt in front of Jens, untied his rope belt and pulled down his black trousers to his ankles. Belinda immediately noticed the tip of the young man's penis dangling below his shirttails. This tantalising revelation developed into a full display when Petta immediately proceeded to lift the shirt at the front and back and knot it so that it stayed out of the way. Belinda stared, and then panicked as she realised she might be caught doing so. But when she glanced at the rest of the audience she saw they were all staring too.

Petta rejoined the group and Thonnig ordered his son to turn and face the tree. The boy did so and, without further bidding, bent over and gripped the

59

trunk. His feet were planted apart as much as the trousers would allow for balance, and Belinda could now enjoy the sight of his swaying balls and dangling penis between his thighs. She would have enjoyed the spectacle better had she been able to strip herself naked and masturbate wildly, and she blushed furiously as she realised what she was thinking. Yet again she was tormented by the inner turmoil that arose from the clash between her middle-class upbringing and her natural lustiness.

Thonnig adjusted his braces and then pulled his arm back. There was a swish and the cane sped to the boy's bottom where it made contact across both buttocks with a startling crack. Jens grunted as the red stripe appeared to reflect the light of the setting sun. Thonnig drew his arm back once more, there was another whistling swish and this time the cane cut across the crease beneath his buttocks. He jerked forward at the cruel impact, and Belinda noticed the women grip their husbands by the arm or shoulder.

The caning continued for a full five minutes until Jens' backside was completely red. It ended when Thonnig suddenly turned and marched back into the camp without a word. His wife jumped up and hurried after him, followed immediately by the three other couples. Belinda watched as each pair hastily clambered into their wagons.

Helle hurried over to Jens to console him. Belinda joined them. Jens himself turned and stared defiantly at his father's wagon. Belinda looked back at the now silent camp. It was as though the occupants had vanished into thin air.

'Now they copulate,' said Helle angrily by way of explanation. 'The founder of our religion decreed that married couples may only enjoy the pleasures of the flesh immediately after they have chastised a sinner. We must wait here and Jens must stand like this in silence until we are summoned back after they have all finished.'

Above the increasing chorus of crickets Belinda heard the wagons creaking and the occasional grunt and short shriek coming from the direction of the camp. Helle said she was going for a walk as she found it too distressing to see poor Jens standing there exposed and aching, and Belinda told her to be careful and said she would stay with him until she returned.

As Helle's slender black-robed form faded into the gathering dusk Belinda sat on the rich grass at Jens' feet and gazed quietly to the west. She wondered if she would ever reach her goal and a happier life. Thoughts of her family made her feel sad and lonely, but even more determined to be successful in her quest. She wondered what dreams Jens had and turned to ask, only to find his lovely semi-erect penis bobbing just inches from her instantly blushing face.

'Oh,' she squealed as a not unwelcome tingle of excitement shot through the soles of her feet and up her legs to her quim. 'What are you doing?' she blundered stupidly. Jens said nothing and continued to stare stoically ahead. Motivated by the desire to comfort – and the desire churning in the pit of her stomach – Belinda stroked his calf uncertainly. Judging by his lack of admonishment she was not breaking any of the sect's rules by doing this; indeed, the only reaction was a healthy surge of his penis that brought it aiming directly at her spellbound face. Although it was still not fully erect she was overwhelmed with a desire to feel it in her mouth. With increasing confidence she slid her hand up the back of his leg to caress his bruised and burning

61

bottom. He quietly sucked in air at her gentle touch. Looking up at him with wide eyes, expecting him to call for help or order her to desist at any moment, she stroked around to the front of his thigh. She worked carefully, as though not wanting to startle a beautiful wild animal. His chest rose and fell more noticeably. Encouraged, she cupped his balls and weighed their youthful virility. She heard a soft gasp from above, and took that as permission to proceed further. His foreskin rolled back of its own accord and his shiny purple helmet inched towards her waiting mouth. She gripped the base of his turgid column and started to masturbate it slowly but firmly. The helmet disappeared inside the protective foreskin, and then reappeared as her fist slid back towards his belly. A silky pearl oozed from the tip, and Belinda leaned forward to collect it on her tongue. She closed her eyes. He tasted fresh and sweet. Fingers urged against the back of her head and she looked up to see Helle standing beside them. She smiled down and the fingers increased their pressure. Belinda's moist lips peeled apart and the clean male flesh filled her mouth with one smooth movement. She knelt passively while Jens' hips pumped freely back and forth. Fingers stroked her hair and her hollowed cheeks. Helle whispered encouragement in her native tongue. Belinda looked up and watched Helle caress Jens' hairless chest and nipples. They kissed passionately, and Jens twitched and mumbled incoherently into her mouth as Belinda's throat filled with his wonderful sperm.

Sunday was the day both of revelations and of great shocks for Belinda. This was the Sabbath, and it was she alone who rose at the first grim grey light of day to prepare the fire and the breakfasts single-handedly.

62

She was initially quite cheerful about this mammoth day of work, given that she had very little real chores to see to during the week. She had learnt that the group could not use their hands on a Sunday for anything except such basic matters as eating, climbing in and out of the wagon, and purely religious topics.

As she hummed to herself her mind once again returned to Friday night, when she had consoled the beaten Jens. She felt her clitoris tingle as she remembered that long cock and its healthy meaty taste, but she had also been intrigued to notice that his hands were quite chunky, whereas those that had molested her in the night had been distinctly of a slender form, just as Thonnig's were. But in spite of all her experiences in life, she found it hard to accept that such a devout man could have done such a thing. Perhaps he had done it in his sleep?

Her thoughts were interrupted by Thonnig himself appearing and climbing down from his wagon, the first of the group to appear that morning. He was dressed of course, since they all slept in their clothes on the trail. She blushed as he approached, sure that he had been reading her thoughts.

'Come, please,' he said, and walked out of the square to the greenery beside the trail.

Belinda followed nervously, and when he stopped she caught him up.

'I need to urinate,' he said in his guttural Danish voice.

Belinda stared at him in astonishment. He looked irritated and pointed to his fly.

'We cannot use our hands,' he said stiffly. 'At home it is easy, we go naked in the house from midnight on Saturday to midnight on Sunday, so toilet is not a trouble. But here is not so easy, that is one reason why

63

we have servant, yes?'

Belinda was mortified, but felt she must comply. She stood behind him and reached around to undo his buttons.

'Hurry, please,' he said quietly, and she rummaged inside and pulled out his cock. She knew immediately from where his son Jens had inherited his generous proportions.

In all that had happened in her relatively short life, this was the most humiliating moment so far. Holding a penis was one thing, but to be such a personal body slave as to have to help a sombre religious maniac like Thonnig to urinate was so shameful that Belinda had to squeeze her eyes tightly shut to prevent the tears from rolling as her head pressed against his black smelly jacket.

She aimed his penis away and felt it swell in her hand as it filled and jetted out noisily onto the rich wild grass. It was a long piss and at the end she had to shake it vigorously and put it away again before they walked back into the wagon square together.

Belinda's face was burning as she resumed her chores, and she was aghast at the thought that she would have to do the same – and worse – for the other members of the group. As she toiled away at her forlorn task of scrubbing the cooking pots with cold water and sand, she tensed when she saw one of the women come out of another wagon. But to her relief the chisel-faced female walked out of the square and disappeared for a few minutes. On her return she simply gave Belinda a look of contempt and climbed back into her canvas home.

Obviously, thought Belinda, it's only the men who will require assistance. The women presumably could manage without offending against their strange laws.

But one by one the remaining men of the group surfaced, and they either ignored her or gave a look of scorn as she laboured on a Sunday. In each case they left the square for a couple of minutes and returned, putting the finishing touches to doing up their trouser buttons.

As the last man returned from seeing to himself, Belinda pushed her hair out of her face with the back of her wrist as an angry suspicion gnawed away at her brain. Frowning, she looked round to glare in Thonnig's direction, but she found he was already giving her a worried look and immediately and guiltily averted his gaze as she looked at him. She felt a little satisfaction when she observed a slight flush rise to his gaunt cheeks.

So that was it. He was the monster whose hand had so cruelly tormented her in the night, knowing that his poor son Jens would get the blame if there was a complaint. But his perverted nature had slipped up today; in his desire to use the religion as an excuse to get her to hold his penis in the open air, he had miscalculated grossly by forgetting that the others would inadvertently show him up by not requiring the same service. She felt so sick that she would have walked straight out of the job there and then, but she was in the middle of a wilderness, and she did have to get to California.

The whole group, with the exception of Jens and the girl Helle, were totally obnoxious to Belinda throughout that holy day. They seemed to have saved all the worst jobs for Sunday, and she found herself washing week old stockings and underwear by hand in the icy water that she had to carry from a nearby stream. There was neither time nor timber enough to heat water. She also had to clean the four wagons

65

thoroughly, and received a lot of vicious abuse from each wife in turn at the slightest excuse. The more she tried to please the nastier they became. They had a prayer meeting in the morning, after she had fed them breakfast, and then they all went for a walk to glorify their interpretation of religion.

Only Thonnig's wife Anna stayed behind after the group agreed that their worldly possessions could not be entrusted to such a low form of life as Belinda. This she found to be the most hurtful thing that had been heaped upon her by these people who had treated her so well up to now. She could not understand it and once again she was close to tears as she wrung out the cold laundry in her chapped hands and watched them stroll away.

Anna went into her wagon, and after a few moments Belinda heard her cry, 'Belinda, get in here!'

Fearfully, wondering what minor mistake she had committed when she had cleaned their wagon, Belinda climbed in. She was relieved to see Anna relaxing on the blankets on the plank floor, although she chilled a little at the Danish woman's hostile stare.

'Come!' snapped Anna patting the floor beside her, and Belinda, not having a clue what to expect, sat down beside her mistress.

'No, no, lie down now,' Anna said very crisply.

Belinda, her heart thumping, obeyed and stretched herself flat on her back beside the woman in the cramped covered wagon. For a minute Anna said nothing; only her heavy breathing could be heard. Then she stared into Belinda's eyes. 'We are alone,' she stated.

Belinda nodded cautiously. She was just wondering if she was to receive a sermon aimed at converting her when Anna's right hand shot out, pushed her dress up to her knees and gripped her just above and inside the hemline. She gasped and stared in amazement as Anna's hand tickled its way up her thigh. Those slender fingers with work-roughened hands – they were the ones that had assaulted her in bed that night. It wasn't Thonnig, it was his wife!

Belinda lay shocked and still as those expert hands stroked her thighs before moving on upwards to her fluffy and, she realised with a feeling of self-loathing, excited vagina. Four coarse fingertips danced lightly up and down her crack and toyed with her clitoris. The woman's skilled fingers quickly allayed Belinda's terror and disgust, and she became quite aroused and surrendered meekly as Anna leaned over her and pressed her lips to hers. As the kiss intensified so did the electrifying tickling. But then, just as Belinda had abandoned all mental protest, Anna pressed her mouth down violently and rammed her tongue into Belinda's throat. This served to stifle our weary traveller's protests as Anna's plier-like fingers crushed the lips of her vulva as they had before. Anna removed her lips from Belinda's, but placed an earthy hand over her mouth to stop her screaming as the spiteful torture of her gentlest parts continued ruthlessly. This was far worse than the previous attack, for Anna had no witnesses to concern herself about. Her interest in torture was very well defined; she was only preoccupied with inflicting as much pain as possible with her fingers on the one part of the young woman's body, and this she did with a furious gusto.

Suddenly she stopped and, pulling her own dress high, threw her legs over Belinda, wriggled up her body and planted her sex over the suffering female lips beneath. Belinda could scarcely breath with the weight of that fanny pressing on her mouth, and she sucked vigorously to make her come – and go – as quickly as possible.

The pious hypocrite did indeed come very quickly, making a noise like a bear that had just lost its honey. That over, she stood up and told Belinda to get out. But as our poor Englishwoman went to leave the wagon Anna slipped a hand up the back of her dress, fondled her bottom and hissed coldly and bewilderingly, 'You will suffer for that, you dirty little Jezebel!'

With emotions a mixture of fear and unrequited sexual arousal, Belinda was once again close to crying as she resumed her chores, this time having to endure the woman's bullying commands to work harder until, at last, the rest of the group returned.

In the middle of the afternoon most of the party had retired for a snooze, and Belinda was somewhat relieved when Thonnig and his wife approached as she was attempting to saw some logs single-handedly. They ordered her to stop work and to walk with them.

They strolled into a nearby deciduous wood, the heat of the afternoon sun diffused by the roof of broad leaves, and they sauntered in silence until they found a small green clearing by a tiny but fast-flowing brook.

'We talk of a personal matter; that is why we leave the group now.'

Belinda wondered about what Thonnig was talking.

'My poor wife has told me of your devilish attack on her while the two of you were alone.'

Belinda was horrified at this unjust statement, but Thonnig continued.

'And I was so outraged that I told her something I had rashly decided to keep a secret for your sake; of how you sneaked up behind me and grabbed my…' he pointed to his groin, 'saying you would hold it for me in case it offended the rules of the Sabbath for me to do it myself.'

Belinda was outraged, but too frightened to protest.

'So,' spoke Anna, 'we decide to teach you manners and to teach you that the lusts of the flesh are not always so nice.'

And without further explanation Thonnig pulled out his wicked looking sheath knife. Belinda almost died of fright, but the knife was not for her. Instead he went to a branch and cut off a knobbly stick, long thick and whippy. She then watched with astonishment as the husband and wife stripped naked until they wore only their stern expressions. Anna's breasts were as impressive as her husband's long cock, and Belinda could not help thinking that her vagina was somehow unusually attractive as its lips peeped through the covering of blonde pubic hair. Both bodies were strong and slender, and Belinda felt a stirring in her depths as she looked at them.

Her poetic thoughts were shattered when the couple suddenly grabbed her and pulled her long dress up over her head and off. She still had no underclothes to her name, and stood facing them in only her boots. Thonnig spun her around and pushed her against the rough bark of a tree while his wife went to the other side. Once there she reached around, took hold of Belinda's wrists and held her bare body tight to the trunk.

Belinda knew what was coming – and it did. Thonnig's knobbly cane swished spitefully and stung the top of her right thigh. There was a pause, and then she heard the swish again just in time to brace herself as the next stripe was laid on her left thigh. Anna pulled her tighter against the rough tree and Belinda's yoni rubbed harshly against the coarse bark. Her nipples were in almost as much agony as her thighs as they rubbed against the roughness of the tree.

There was a moment's respite for Belinda as the naked Thonnig strode to the other side of the tree. His wife maintained her grip on Belinda, and her devoted husband gave Anna six slashes of the stick on her bottom, legs and back until she screamed. He returned to Belinda and felt her weals before administering a further four cuts to her thighs and, horror of horrors, the backs of her knees.

'Save some for the main meeting, my husband,' said Anna, which puzzled Belinda until Thonnig explained.

'After prayers tonight we will consider the fact that you have committed multiple and blatant blasphemies all the day long. This is what I would have told you when you joined us, but you did not care. As long as you had a job going westwards you were happy. Tonight you will be tied to a wagon wheel and every member of the group will beat you in their own way. You may look forward to sticks, straps, whips, hands... everything until we feel you have purged your sins. Then we will leave you tied up until morning while we go to bed. Is good, eh?'

Belinda did not answer that rhetorical question, and Anna released her wrists. As Belinda, her face as red as her legs, turned around she was taken aback to see that Thonnig had a huge erection, and that Anna was smiling at it.

'Please kneel,' ordered Thonnig quietly, and his wife encouraged Belinda to her knees by pressing on her shoulders. With Anna behind her, the kneeling Belinda watched Thonnig and his powerful penis approach. He brushed its tip against the poor young woman's cheeks. Belinda looked over it into his cold

70

eyes.

'I thought it was only each other you could have sex with after correcting a sinner,' she said with unaccustomed defiance.

Thonnig's eyebrows rose and he glanced at his wife. 'You already know something about our beliefs then,' he said as a simple statement. 'Many interpret it that way. Our founder and mentor, Pers Laurentzen, wrote that a married couple may only have sex immediately after correcting a sinner. Anna and I have studied that passage many times, and we have concluded that he does not say a married couple must have sex only with each other after correcting a wrongdoer; just that they can only have sex.'

Yes, thought Belinda, not for the first time have men and women interpreted religious teachings to their own ends, but her cynicism was interrupted as Anna's strong fingers squeezed into her cheeks so that she opened her mouth to ease the discomfort, and her free hand fed her husband's eager penis between the warm wet lips. As the solid flesh pumped inside Belinda, Anna masturbated it, slowly at first but then with increasing frenzy until all at once there was an extra powerful thrust that almost choked Belinda and her mouth was filled with salty liquid as the muscular Dane orgasmed between her lips and his wife's hand. The couple kept that cock inside her mouth until it had fully subsided, and in the meantime poor Belinda had no choice but to swallow every last drop.

'Our fellows in God will not interpret the laws to permit me to do this to you again tonight,' said Thonnig coldly. 'But please be assured that we will both be looking forward to giving you another – and this time unrestrained – whacking by the light of the campfire.'

71

Belinda hung her head sadly at the turn of events, but moments later her attention was drawn as Thonnig cursed and Anna screamed. She looked up and almost fainted with fright. Stalking into the tiny clearing were half a dozen painted and near-naked savage Indians, with alarming bows and arrows aimed at the naked threesome.

Chapter Four

Belinda's tragedy filled life was about to come to its final horrible conclusion. Of this she was certain as she rode into the small Indian camp, mounted on their leader's horse, with him sitting behind her.

After surprising them in the woods, the fiendishly handsome savages had chased Thonnig and Anna away without letting them gather up their clothes. They seemed to think such a joke was far more fun than actually killing them.

But Belinda had lost all hope of their sense of humour saving her. She had been snatched by rough hands and dragged along the prickly ground through the woods to where the small patrol had their horses hidden. One of the brutes had thrown her dress at her and after slipping it on she had ridden harshly and painfully on the unsaddled horse for several hours before reaching the bonfire-lit camp. Throughout this time the leader on whose horse she was riding had kept his hand up her dress and his middle finger firmly planted inside her shaft. The bouncing horse had converted this position into a blend of agony and ecstasy, both elements being heightened by the Indian biting cruelly into her shoulders from time to time and ramming his rock-hard cock hard against her backbone.

The reason the terror-stricken young woman had for thinking her life was not to last much longer, in spite of the apparent leniency towards her religious tormentors, was the hell-like scene that revealed itself as her eyes became accustomed to the fire lit gloom.

The small camp was in a clearing in the dense

forest, and consisted of a half dozen badly erected wigwams amongst the surrounding trees. A charred human skull lay at the edge of the fire, and an arm bone and one or two other human parts could also be discerned in the smoky dimness. But the real clinching horror was the upright frames of timber and leather thongs, about six of them, from which were suspended bodies in various states of decay. The mixture of male and female, Indian and white men – according to their tattered clothing – was enough to simultaneously nauseate Belinda and to terrify all hope from her fear-frozen mind.

As they wheeled into the centre of the camp a dozen women and a few other men ran out to greet them. The absence of any children was a further chilling factor for Belinda; this was clearly not a camp of happy families, and her despair deepened dramatically.

The screaming women in their stinking animal skin tunics gathered around the returning patrol. The leading savage pulled his finger from beneath Belinda's skirt. He threw her to the ground and wheeled away with a blood-chilling scream, leaving her to the female savages. They fell on her at once and countless hands explored and tormented her cruelly. Some were fascinated by her fine chestnut hair, and stroked it and then yanked it fiercely. She felt hands inside the top of her dress, apparently to feel if her breasts were any different from their own, and to test if the nipples were sensitive to vicious pinching. A pair of the screeching she-devils raised her dress to poke and squeeze her poor labia. Another grabbed one of the terrified Belinda's hands and shoved it under her own tunic where she pressed it hard against the coarse hairs that covered her genitalia.

Belinda's screams and struggles seemed to serve to

74

excite the howling human pack to a fiendish frenzy, until she was just a mixed mass of pain and pleasure as their hands roamed, tickled, stung, tore and scratched at her flesh...

At last they exhausted themselves and stood back to study their prize. As they towered contemptuously over her, she saw that some of the men had been standing and watching gleefully. They were all identically dressed; naked except for a leather loincloth at back and front with the sides of their thighs fully exposed. Their sleek black hair hung halfway down their backs. As she stared up at their muscular bodies she realised with a shock that she was actually thinking how easy it would be to put one's hand up under those loincloths. She was also startled by the awareness that, the likelihood of death apart, her tormented body was actually beginning to enjoy the cruel attentions she was attracting from everyone she met in this fierce land. Nonetheless, she decided that she should never admit this disturbing reality lest it incited her molesters to further horrors which might leave her mutilated or even – she shuddered as she glanced at the bodies on the frames – executed.

Suddenly it seemed that that was to be her immediate fate, for the feathered leader who had brought her in appeared and shouted a command. At once she was seized and dragged sobbing to a frame in the clearing where her dress was removed with surprising care. She was forced up against the timber frame and coarse leather thongs were attached to her wrists and ankles so she could be tied to each corner of the structure with her arms and legs stretched wide. She was facing the fire and could feel the heat on her naked front. Her heart pounded as she heard the rhythmic beating of some tom-toms, and the crowd fell

75

silent. A female appeared from the painted wigwam behind Belinda and up went a cheer. The ugly flat-faced squaw walked around to the front of Belinda and the English girl saw she had some sort of short stick in her hands. She stopped near to Belinda, and then another female approached the first, carrying half a melon skin which acted as a container for a large dollop of some sort of grease.

The crone with the stick sat on the ground by the bowl of grease, and the small crowd moved closer with an excited murmur. Belinda temporarily forgot about dying as she saw what the stick really was. It was a phallus that was perfectly fashioned out of shiny black plaited leather. The length of her forearm and almost as thick, its full and flawless head appeared to be made of a polished stone set snugly in amongst the thongs that made up its shaft. At the other end the leather opened out into a bag that was filled with sand and whose finely grained leather surface gave a remarkable impersonation of a scrotum.

The black-eyed crone proudly held the phallus aloft and the savages cheered and screeched. She looked at Belinda and grinned in a sickening way. She reached into the bowl of grease, scooped up a handful, and started massaging it into the leather penis. The crowd shouted with ribald delight as she made much of masturbating the baton, and she rubbed more and more grease into it until it glistened obscenely in the firelight.

When she appeared satisfied with her work she tested it by lying back on the ground, lifting her tunic and inserting the slippery length slowly inside herself for about a third of its length. Belinda was disgusted, and then she struggled fearfully against the bonds as the crone withdrew it with a cackle, stood up, and approached her.

The beat of the drums intensified and the gathered savages shrieked excitedly as the crone stroked the gleaming phallus up Belinda's thighs until its lustrous cold tip pressed against the entrance to her vagina. A man moved into the light of the fire, and Belinda numbly saw he was carrying a short thick whip, like a flexible black billiard cue. He showed it to Belinda, and then moved behind her. She knew what to expect. It was pointless to protest.

The savages fell silent and gawped. The old crone pressed the artificial monstrosity firmly against Belinda's defenceless vulva. It was held there as the first agonising lash struck her back, and as she jerked forward its huge head opened her and slipped partially inside. She gasped at the intrusion, closed her eyes, and braced herself bravely for the next stroke of the whip. As it bit into her shoulder she spasmed again and the monster slid deeper and deeper.

The tormentor with the whip steadily and unhurriedly worked his way down her back to her firm white buttocks. The enormous dildo was fully inserted and the crone slowly fucked her captive with it. Her raven eyes sparkled evilly in the shadowy light. Belinda barely felt the vicious whip now; she was totally absorbed by the leather cock sliding up and down inside her and stimulating her swollen clitoris. The shiny stone head also gave her a wondrous yet almost overwhelming feeling of satisfying fullness. She was almost delirious from the excess of physical sensations when the crone cruelly pulled the phallus away, leaving her empty and gasping for more. The beating stopped too, both of her back and of the tom-toms. She breathed deeply and tried to calm herself, but suddenly a hard body pushed fiercely against her

77

from behind. She felt a leather loincloth, but then with a fumble this was raised and a large but real erection pressed between her tender buttocks. Another Indian whooped and jumped in front of her. He lifted his covering and proudly displayed his cock. It was powerfully erect too, and Belinda felt her legs weaken from a cocktail of trepidation and desire. The savage behind her seemed content to prod his helmet against her bottom. She swooned with unwanted desire, and through lowered eyelids watched the savage in front approach and enter her fully with one irresistible movement. She tried to deny him the satisfaction of knowing how beautiful he felt, but it was useless. She screamed with ecstasy as she came more fully than ever before in her young life. The Indian leered triumphantly and rammed harder and harder until he exploded inside her clutching depths.

All of Belinda's fears were gone and forgotten as the savage orgy continued through the night. She was enjoyed by all the strong young warriors as she stood tied in the frame, and was also enjoyed by most of the women. She even had the pleasant change of watching some of the younger squaws being stripped and lashed with the same instrument that had been used on her. She was proudly amused to see that they did not take it as well as she had.

Gradually the orgiastic mayhem subsided, and the camp fell into a state of drug induced and satiated slumber.

Belinda opened her eyes and was astonished to find that daylight was just breaking. She had actually managed to fall asleep in her horribly uncomfortable position, and she now felt the dawn chilling her naked body. As she looked around she saw the tribe were asleep on the ground in various positions.

Suddenly she remembered the bodies in the other frames around the camp's perimeter, and her state of arousal was instantly replaced by unmitigated terror. If the bodies had looked ghostly in the firelight, in the grey of morning they looked positively stomach churning as the stark reality of their mutilated and rotting state was revealed. It took every ounce of willpower to avoid screaming hysterically as she realised she too would soon look like those wretched cadavers.

In desperation she tugged and tugged against the bonds that held her, and her heart pounded when she felt one thong give slightly. Scarcely able to believe there was any chance of successfully freeing herself, she continued giving the strap sharp tugs in different directions. It soon fell away, and her hand was free. Terrified that she might have been seen she watched the sleeping Indians, trying to control her breathing, which sounded loud enough to wake the whole state. All was well, and she was just able to reach her left wrist and undo the bond there. It was then a matter of seconds to release her ankles. She felt physically sick as she picked up her dress and tiptoed stiffly towards the surrounding trees. If she was spotted now she would not get another chance and would end up dying like those other poor souls. Fortunately there were no dogs to raise the alarm, and the horses were on the farthest side of the camp.

Fighting down the terror-inspired nausea lest the sound of her vomiting aroused one of the sleepers, she made it to the cover of the woods. She turned and peered back anxiously through the greenery, but the camp was still quiet. It's a shame to leave such

79

sophisticated company, she thought bitterly, but I really must be heading west. She didn't let fear turn into excitement, however, until she had tiptoed for a few hundred yards and then, still naked and with her dress clutched in one hand, she ran for her life, not knowing where she was going but not caring as long as it was away from that hideous camp and its demonic inhabitants.

Chapter Five

Once again Belinda was on horseback, but this time there were some significant differences compared with her last ride.

For one, she was sitting behind the rider instead of in front of him, and secondly this rider was a civilised rancher who was taking her to safety rather than torture and death. It's the little things in life that make all the difference, thought Belinda with a smile as they galloped along.

Tom McLaren was a big man, both in character and physique. Well built without a hint of fat, he was returning from a successful trip where he had arranged a buyer for as many cattle as he and his neighbours could deliver to St Joseph.

He was dressed in the traditional cattle rancher's style; light brown leather waistcoat, check shirt, denim trousers and leather chaps, topped off by a black wide-brimmed hat. He had almost run Belinda down when his black stallion and accompanying packhorse had come galloping around a bend to find her in the middle of the track by the woods.

She had told him of her horrible experience with the Indians, and he had been very concerned. He assured her that all the regular Indians were very peaceful just then and that what she described sounded more like an infamous pack of heathen murderers that had been exiled by their own people, who called them the Devil Men. He was amazed at her skill and fortune in contriving to escape, but was not surprised to hear the Indians had allowed the Danish couple to go. It seems it was the traditional thing for the Devil Men to take only one prisoner; the youngest and best looking woman or man in a group.

At first Tom's main attraction was that he was going some six hundred miles in a westerly direction, a journey he said would take around twelve days of hard riding. She liked Tom, and had decided to give his offer of a job as housekeeper helping his wife a trial run. If it worked out, fine. If it did not it would at least be a sophisticated break in her Spartan quest for her uncle.

For five days Belinda sat behind Tom, her bare vagina below the long dress pressed hard against the constant movement of the horse's broad back and her hands wrapped around Tom's waist, just above his thick leather belt. To her surprise he made no moves towards seducing her, let alone beating her as seemed to be the standard in this harsh country. When they slept on the uncomfortable ground at night he kept well away and always respected her privacy.

All of this had a reverse effect on our heroine, who had become accustomed to sexual abuse and had now begun to expect it. Her desire for him grew and grew, and she began to find her frustration caused her more pain and misery than any of the beatings to which she had become inured. She resorted to masturbating beneath the coarse blankets he'd loaned her from his ample panniers, but her agony continued. Had there been an older and wiser person to confide in she would have learnt that her turmoil, confusion, and inner conflicts were hardly surprising, given that she was not yet twenty and had seen her secure and comfortable home life destroyed and replaced with vagrancy and cruelty.

By mid-afternoon on the sixth day, having been riding since dawn at quite a fast pace over easy country, the constant rubbing of the horse's back into the apex of her thighs and the feel of Tom's strong stomach beneath her palms finally conquered her feminine shyness – but only after she had wrestled at length with her high moral standards. These somehow seemed to matter less when the two of them were alone in the wilderness; it was as if they were the only people left on earth and could formulate their own code of ethics.

She let her hand rest on his belt as they rode along, but then allowed it to slip slowly downwards, in a gentle search for his penis. She did not have to look far. Almost immediately below the belt she discovered a lump and her heart thumped as she realised it was the tip of his cock, which was clearly erect. Thus encouraged, she moved her fingers down a little further and pressed them against the shaft. Tom said nothing, but he throbbed beneath the denim and her grip as she tightened her fingers around the bulge. It felt as enormous as she had imagined it to be whilst beneath her blankets over the last few nights.

They rode along in silence and she became bolder, feeling and crushing his rod all over, her chaste principles completely if temporarily abandoned. She didn't care if she did feel angry with herself afterwards. She pressed herself tighter against the horse's back and squeezed her thighs against its sides. At last, with tremendous difficulty, she managed to undo Tom's brass-buttoned fly, and feverishly plunged her hand inside to feel his bare thighs and that truly promising member. She pulled it out and blissfully rode along massaging him slowly but firmly in the warm open air. She found that if she kept her hand tightly wrapped around it but completely still, the movements of the beast beneath them caused it to pump up and down in her fist. Tom didn't make a sound, until suddenly he emitted a taut groan and Belinda felt his hot seed spurt between her bunched fingers and trickle over her hand and wrist. She milked him gently until he was coming no more. She then gathered up her torn and dirty dress at the hem and, reaching in front of Tom again, dutifully wiped him dry. She then gripped his shoulder with one hand, slipped her other under the dress, and teased herself furiously until she bit her lip and shuddered to her own wonderful orgasm.

They rode on, and not a word was said.

To Belinda's disappointment nothing was said that night either, apart from the normal conversation, and he once again left her untouched at bedtime. But the next day – and each of the following days – she repeated the performance, first masturbating him as they rode along and then finishing herself off behind him. How strange, thought Belinda, that he hadn't even offered to spank her. Perhaps that phase of her life was finally behind her. Tears rolled down her cheeks as she realised that here was the first decent man she had met in a long, long time and that she, the highly principled music teacher, instead of appreciating his goodness had acted as the filthy defiler.

At about five o'clock on the tenth afternoon they rode over the brow of a hill and there was Tom's ranch below, in a grassy plain with a river flowing through it against a backdrop of snow-capped mountains.

Tom dismounted for a minute to admire the view and to point out, quite unnecessarily, his homestead, a big log cabin with many windows and a porch that was bigger than her room in Liverpool. Other buildings were scattered about the immediate area, and of course there were cows everywhere. It all looked completely magical as the sun started to set behind the mountain peaks, making the snowy tips glow ruby red.

Tom looked at her firmly. 'Belinda, before we join my wife,' he said in his easy fashion, 'there's something I just got to do. Would you mind coming back down the hill a way to those trees? I would prefer that my wife doesn't see this.'

Belinda's heart leapt so hard it nearly knocked her off the horse. Oh heavens, she thought, he is actually going to make love to me as a farewell present. But now that she was within sight of his home and about to meet his wife, who would clearly be as wonderful a woman as he was a man, her passion had faded and her righteous standards had restored themselves in her heart and soul. Her uncharacteristic passions and behaviour during that long horseback ride were now fading as fast as any nightmare upon awakening. And yet she felt she could not refuse him, for amongst other things, he had taken her about a quarter of her way west and had also offered her a civilised job with his wife for as long as it suited her to stay. She had little option.

'Whatever you say, Tom. I've loved your company, and you probably saved my life by getting me away from that Indian area. I will come with you.'

Before she had finished the sentence he was leading the horse, with her still on it, back down the hill. He stopped by a clump of trees and tied its rein to one of them. Belinda's heart was thumping as he looked up at her legs; she had lifted her skirt up high to let the breeze in.

Then he held out his hand and helped her down. He stood facing her with his hands resting on her waist, and she gazed up into his eyes.

85

'Belinda,' he said carefully. 'I sure enjoyed what you did to me every day as we rode along.'

She smiled at him, the warmth of her clitoris increasing with a combination of anticipation and the memory of his fine cock in her hand.

'Trouble is, I oughtn't to have let you do it, me being happily married and all.'

Belinda was about to reassure him it was nothing, but he continued.

'So I figured, the best way to stop me feeling all bad about it is for you to admit it was your fault, because I sure wouldn't have started nothing like that on my own, and then for me to make up for it by punishing you. Please do that for me, Belinda, or I'll never live with myself.'

He spoke with such sincerity – and what he said was true. She had been the one to start it, and if one more whacking in her life could help a thoroughly good man like Tom feel better, then she would just have to take it. Anyway, the six hundred mile ride was worth a lot more than some of the miserable payments she had received in Liverpool for being beaten without any tender feelings being involved.

'I'm sorry, Tom,' she whispered nervously. 'I played on your masculine sensuality. It was a cheap trick and I had no right to make you feel bad or to jeopardise your happy marriage.' She looked down and added softly, 'If punishing me will make you feel better, Tom, then so be it.'

Tom nodded grimly and pulled his riding crop from its sheath on the side of the saddle. Belinda felt her bottom contract at the sight and thought of it.

'Stand by the side of the horse, please,' he commanded firmly. 'Face the saddle and lift your skirts.'

86

Belinda was quite happy to expose herself to him. Her bare vulva caught his eye, but he looked back at her face immediately as she turned obediently. She was taken a little by surprise when his strong arms wrapped around her thighs, but then he heaved her up and lay her across the saddle so her head was dangling over the other side and her rump was high in the air. She was reasonably well balanced, but caught hold of the stirrup for extra security. She felt the breeze play around her soft buttocks, and then Tom said gruffly, 'You ready?'

She nodded, although he could not have seen that from where he was standing. She heard a swish and gave a little short scream of expectancy... but nothing happened.

'It's all right,' said Tom, 'I was just testing and getting the feel of my own strength. I don't want to be too hard on you.'

And with that the crop stung across both buttocks with exceptional viciousness. He clearly did not know his own strength if that was meant to be reasonably gentle.

'Say you're sorry, Belinda,' he drawled.

'Sorry!' she cried as the pain surged through her body and then receded to its red-hot source.

The riding crop again whistled through the air and landed in exactly the same place across her bottom. That hurt.

'No,' she screamed, 'I'm sorry!'

This little ritual was repeated ten more times to a total of twelve. Each strike was in almost exactly the same place, with her pleas for clemency getting louder each time. The Indians had terrified her, but even they had not hurt her so much as this strong man with his unerring accuracy. But in spite of the pain she resolutely stayed in position until he had finished.

Expecting a thirteenth stroke, she flinched as she felt his hand touch her bottom gently and heard him say, 'Get down now.'

She slid stiffly off the horse, letting her dress drop back into place, and stared at him red-faced and with tears in her eyes. She half hated him and half loved him.

'This is all your fault,' he said solemnly.

'Yes, well, it was,' she retorted sulkily. 'But now I've been punished accordingly.'

'No,' he said, and patted the front of his denims to demonstrate his giant erection. 'I mean this.'

The heat from Belinda's bottom immediately rushed to her vagina.

'First time I've seen a beautiful woman as bare as that since I got married, let alone had the close contact of whacking her backside. Now you've gone and filled me with craving.' He undid his belt and then his jeans. 'I can't go home like this,' he continued, 'so you better give me some relief.' He pulled his penis out into the open.

Belinda had felt it yet never actually seen it, but it was as handsome as she had imagined it to be.

'Lead me over to that tree,' he said a little hoarsely.

Belinda, suitably chastened and obedient, meekly took his penis firmly in her hand and used it to guide him to the large tree he had indicated. She stood with her back against the rough trunk and pulled his cock closer until it was pressing at her mons Veneris through the flimsy dress. Suddenly consumed with desire she feverishly hoisted her skirts high above her waist once again. Tom gripped the backs of her thighs, lifted her off the ground, and squashed her stinging backside against the knarled tree.

The tip of his penis probed at the highly sensitised lips of her vulva. She tried to suck him in. He moaned and pressed more firmly. She felt the pattern of the bark imprinting itself on her tender bottom, and gave a scream of absolute bliss as she felt his incredible instrument ply its glorious way past her clitoris to fill her until she felt she would surely burst. He kissed her fervently and fucked her with great passion, his bodily spasms increasing with each smooth thrust. Her head lolled from side to side against the tree. Tom panted and strained, and Belinda mumbled deliriously as she squeezed her thighs around his hips and jerked up and down on his erection.

When they came they came together, and she felt as if the combined force of the two orgasms had forced her right through the tree. And then they slumped together down the trunk until Tom was kneeling, and she felt him pulse the last vestiges of sperm into her.

Before they moved off down the hill Tom half-turned in his saddle.

'Belinda,' he said like a shy boy. 'I sure hope you understand I did everything I could to be faithful to my darling wife.'

Belinda felt a surge of sentiment and fought back the tears as she whispered, 'Of course, Tom. Of course I do.'

As they moved away Tom reached back and squeezed her leg; a simple and heart-warming act that filled Belinda with immense affection for the man.

This new heaven continued to augur well when Tom introduced his wife Rachel. She was a big blonde in her thirties, and so beautiful that Belinda fully understood his faithfulness, even if it was only partial. She was a bright and cheerful woman; a real farmer's

89

wife, except there was nothing homely about her face or her figure. Her blondeness was emphasised by a long pale blue dress, and her hair was delightfully curled in a most expensive way. The whole home was equally stylish; everything simple, nothing pretentious, but all of the finest quality.

Rachel greeted Belinda warmly, and expressed shock and sympathy as Tom repeated Belinda's tragic tale from her landing in Virginia right up to her night with the Indians. He also told her that he had asked Belinda to consider staying on as housekeeper, and that his business trip had been eminently successful. So successful, he went on, that he had to carry on riding straight after he had eaten to tell all his neighbours to start rounding up and sorting out their stock for the big drive east that was going to make them all rich men. He would be away for another two days or so. Rachel was disappointed but did not complain, and she was bright and chatty in an intelligent way all through dinner, with Belinda feeling human once again having bathed in hot scented water and dressed in a fresh wine-coloured dress that Rachel had dug out for her. When Belinda agreed to accept the position as housekeeper Rachel clapped her hands with delight and beamed brightly at her throughout the meal.

When the finely cooked steak and potato dinner was over Belinda and Rachel cleared the table while Tom sat by the log fire pensively smoking a cigar. Eventually he rose, gathered his hat, kissed Rachel warmly and bade farewell to Belinda, saying he would see them both in a few days.

Belinda sighed contentedly, but received a terrible shock when Rachel closed the front door and turned back to her. The warm smile was gone and there was a somewhat sinister glint in her eyes. 'Is something the matter, Rachel?' she asked in bewilderment.

'What makes you think I need a housekeeper?' she sneered, making Belinda blink in astonishment.

'B-but...' stammered Belinda, 'Tom told me you needed help... and he offered me the job.' She was truly alarmed by this turn of events. Rachel pulled a dining chair out from the table and coldly told her to sit. As she respectfully obeyed Rachel pulled out another chair and placed it in front of the first, but did not sit herself. Instead she stood close to the confused Belinda, staring down at her.

'You want to know why Tom gave you a job?'

Belinda shook her head, and then nodded; she didn't know what she wanted. She started to speak and then judged it best not to. Rachel ignored her anyway.

'A few months ago me and Tom got drunk here one night, and he got me telling him all my dirty little secret thoughts. Know what I mean?'

Belinda nodded. She knew of such thoughts, but did not know what form Rachel's took.

'I told him that back east before I met him I used to have a certain bit of fun every now and so often. And while I loved him and my life on the ranch dearly, I sure did hanker after some of that fun.'

Belinda wondered what the 'certain bit of fun' was, as she looked up at Rachel's full bosom and deep cleavage bulging attractively from the low-cut dress. Moreover, what did it have to do with her?

'You see, Belinda, I'm a normal healthy woman, and I have my needs – especially when Tom's away on his long rides.'

'What...' Belinda hardly dared ask, 'what sort of needs?'

'I adore beautiful women,' Rachel answered

confidently.

Belinda's jaw dropped.

'I adore spanking beautiful women,' Rachel qualified her particular penchant.

Belinda was utterly speechless. She had been spanked many times of course, and two of her regulars in England had been women... but Rachel?!

'So you see,' continued the confident woman without respite, 'that is why my husband offered you the job; to be my beautiful plaything.'

Belinda's head was in a spin.

'Well?' demanded Rachel. 'What d'you say?'

Belinda was actually relieved that she wasn't having to face the wrath of a jealous wife, and she had no desire to swap this warm and comfortable ranch for the hostile night outside. She looked up at her domineering host and nodded.

Rachel's eyes lit up triumphantly. 'Excellent!' she breathed, and went to a corner of the room. She moved aside a casual table and lifted a floorboard. She reached in and retrieved a short cane made of tightly rolled black leather. As she returned to the uncertain Belinda she also picked up a wooden hairbrush from another small table and, from a drawer, a leather strap that looked as if it were made from one of Tom's belts.

Rachel sat on the vacant chair before Belinda and put the instruments on the dining table. They sat facing each other with their knees almost touching through their long dresses.

To begin with Rachel simply stared at Belinda, until the latter became embarrassed and lowered her gaze. She sighed sharply, making Belinda look up again.

'Show me your legs,' she ordered quietly but firmly.

Belinda nervously gripped the dress and, staring solemnly at her mistress, gathered the material up to her knees.

'I said show me your legs!' hissed Rachel, and Belinda hastily and wisely bunched the rustling skirts up around her narrow waist so that her white knickers were on display as well as her legs. Rachel breathed slowly and savoured the beautiful sight. Her bosom swelled even more precariously over her dress. She reached forward and pushed the young woman's legs apart. Despite her trepidation a thrill coursed through Belinda's body. She felt a powerful attraction to this strong and beautiful lady of the house, and the implements on the table took her breath away.

Rachel started to explore the silky insides of Belinda's thighs, staring deep into her plaything's eyes as she did so. Belinda luxuriated in the sensual attentions, favourably comparing sitting in the warm with a bisexual hedonist to hanging from a frame in an encampment of murderous savages. She moaned softly, closed her eyes, and leaned back as far as the upright chair would allow. Rachel's hands drifted further along her thighs towards the crisp white cotton and the succulent promise hiding within.

'This what you liked Tom doing to you?' she coaxed, and when Belinda opened her eyes to answer she saw that Rachel had a hand resting on the leather strap.

'He didn't touch me anywhere,' she whispered desperately.

'You liar,' insisted Rachel in a calm but chilling tone. She cruelly held the strap for her victim to see. 'Cane for long range. Strap for medium range. And brush for close range.'

Before Belinda could ponder the science of it all Rachel raised the leather to her shoulder and then lashed it down on a diagonal course that struck the inside of her left thigh. Belinda didn't need to pretend – it was agonising and she howled in despair. She longed to rub her scorched flesh, but Rachel ordered her to keep the dress held high. Again the strap raised, and again it lashed down spitefully. Poor Belinda howled again as tears welled up in her eyes and burst onto her flushed cheeks. Rachel grinned cruelly at the sight of them.

'Stand up, you little temptress!' she hissed.

Belinda rose instantly, sniffling and keeping the skirts gathered beneath her breasts. As she stood with her thighs burning and her clitoris tingling Rachel pulled her close and swapped the strap for the hairbrush. She then tugged the crisp white knickers down and gazed upon her triangle of soft chestnut curls. Inserting a finger she toyed with the juicy clitoris that hid there. She inhaled deeply the sweet scent of her plaything, before turning her around and feasting her eyes on those glorious buttocks. Her fingertips traced the red weals from the whipping Tom had administered, but to Belinda's relief she made no comment.

Then she started using the back of the brush. She worked systematically, spanking each calf in turn and gradually working her way up both legs. Belinda was teetering on the edge of a shattering orgasm when the chastisement abruptly – and to Belinda's secret misery – ceased.

'Take your dress off, darling,' Rachel whispered with a tenderness that totally confused the poor girl. When naked, Rachel made her kneel between her thighs, raised her own blue dress, and dropped it over her plaything's head.

It was warm and dark, and Belinda closed her eyes as hands urged against the back of her head and drew her towards the source of the warmth. Soft thighs caressed her cheeks, and her nose nestled into delicately scented hair.

'Kiss me,' she heard the muffled instruction through the enclosing skirts. She tentatively licked and kissed the moist labia. Slowly relaxing, she was even beginning to enjoy the task and apply herself more diligently when a strip of heat exploded agonisingly across her bare bottom. The cane rained down on her relentlessly and salty tears mingled with Rachel's flowing juices on her tongue. Desperate to appease her tormentor she sucked and sucked and sucked, and did not scream until the very last vicious swipe of that thin rod landed not on her blazing buttocks but on the upturned sole of her foot.

Thankfully, that was the end of the beating, and they made passionate love for another couple of hours before falling asleep. Rachel instructed Belinda not to let on to Tom, but to act as if she really was a housekeeper, just in case that had really been his intention.

When Tom returned two days later, Belinda rather nervously announced that she wished to continue on her trek to find her uncle. She had come to the decision during the second night, following another torrid session with Rachel. It had certainly been an exciting and sexually fulfilling interlude, and she now knew without a doubt that she could take a deal of pain – even though her innate innocence still left her puzzled as to why so many people wanted to treat her in such a way. But she also knew that she wanted more out of life than being stuck on the ranch forever, and she was certainly opposed on principle to voluntarily following a lifestyle based on sexual gratification, especially as she always had great difficulties in saying 'no'.

Rachel was, of course, quietly furious at the loss of Belinda – a dream that could surely never be repeated in that remote wilderness – but could say nothing in front of her mildly disappointed husband. It was obvious now that Rachel had concocted the story about his giving her Belinda as a sexual gift. He wished Belinda luck, and arranged for one of his ranch hands to take her to the nearest neighbour, who would then relay her to the next, and so on until he had helped her as far on her journey as he could.

Chapter Six

The worst thing about the relay of lifts provided by Tom's ranch hand, and the string of neighbours, was that they all insisted on her masturbating them as she sat behind them as the price for taking her in the right direction. But what really sickened her was not having to oblige them all, it was learning from these gleeful men that Tom had told about her behaviour out on the trail, and his message had been quickly passed down the line. Belinda just could not believe that Tom had turned out to be no different to all the others, and she cried several times at the thought, to the great amusement of his fellows.

It was approaching sunset when the last of her long rides dropped her on a rise overlooking what, after such a long time in the wilds, looked like a great metropolis on the scale of Liverpool or Manchester. But as she walked down the hill towards the town she realised it was a relatively small place. Walking along the trail she took in the town as it nestled in the shade of the small range of jagged hills that surrounded it. There appeared to be just one main street going right through the centre. On either side of this was a maze of shacks, stables and narrow dusty lanes, and, on the outskirts at one end, three white villas with small gardens. The main street was a-throng with lively crowds of men and a few women. There was a great deal of noise and jostling and uncouth language. It could almost be, thought Belinda, the meaner part of Liverpool where she had unhappily spent the last year or so after her home life collapsed. She realised with a start that she had barely given her father or brother a thought recently, so wrapped up had she been in her own difficulties, and she immediately dropped to her knees on the stony cactus-strewn ground and whispered a tearful prayer for their wellbeing. Once she had reached her uncle she would not take long in re-establishing contact with them, perhaps even returning home. Or perchance her uncle was so rich he would be easily persuaded to pay off their debts, fines, and compensation and get them released and maybe he would even start them off in a new life. Fortified by these thoughts she determined that she would grit her teeth against all that this cruel land could hurl at her, and do whatever it took to get to her uncle... for her family's sake.

But for now, as she entered the noisy town, her thoughts had to be on herself, for she was hungry, thirsty, homeless and penniless, and was not even sure where she was or how much further she still had to go.

The crowds in the street looked no more charitable than those had in St Joseph. The few women pursed their lips and hurried past with contemptuous looks on their hard faces, whilst those men who took any notice did so in very crude ways, shouting out coarsely suggestive remarks at this sad teenage girl. Some of them even blatantly rubbed their crotches through their dirty denim trousers, more to amuse their friends than to impress her.

Halfway along the dusty street Belinda came to a noisy saloon. The racket coming from within was appalling, although to Belinda's cultured ears the worst of it was the hideous way somebody was attempting to play a piano. But, deciding this might be a good place to seek employment, she took a deep breath, pushed open the batwing doors and entered.

She looked around the smoky saloon

apprehensively. The place was extremely busy and her arrival was scarcely noticed. It was packed with men, mainly sitting around tables and either playing cards in silence or conversing and laughing in loud, bantering and sometimes hysterical ways. Half a dozen waiters in whitish shirts and long aprons moved amongst the tables, occasionally being tripped by jokers with protruding feet. About a dozen glamorous women were making it their business to treat the men with great courtesy, but Belinda was a little saddened to note that some of the customers took advantage of the women's good nature and slapped their bottoms as they passed, and, in a couple of instances, even shot their hands up the back of the girls' long dresses. One of them responded by emptying the offending client's beer over his head to the great amusement of all in the vicinity. Belinda decided the place was a bit rough but nonetheless friendly. If it hadn't been for the scruffy man slouched over the piano and hammering misshapen chords out of it in the most unmelodious way, she could have found the atmosphere almost appealing. She had certainly seen worse in Liverpool.

She conveyed herself to the bar, feeling very self-conscious of her trail-soiled state in comparison with the glamour of the other ladies in the room, and tried to attract the attention of one of the busy bartenders. She hoped they might point her in the direction of gainful and decent employment. She also hoped they might give her a glass of water at least, but she was unable to get any of them to take any notice of her at all. She was almost on the point of crying with fatigue and frustration when a big man turned to her. She gasped as she saw his face. It looked as if it had fought in many wars on the losing side, being heavily scarred and with the whole of the end of the nose missing.

'New round here, ain't you?' he asked in a hoarse voice.

'Yes,' replied Belinda with sweet politeness. It wasn't his fault he looked the way he did. 'I'm rather desperate for money, and was hoping I might be able to earn some here.'

He grinned. 'Shouldn't be too hard, lady,' he wheezed. He looked pointedly at her full and heaving breasts. 'I guess you could play a man a pretty tune, eh?'

Belinda brightened. 'Oh yes, I could do that all right,' she said excitedly, glancing across at the drunken pianist. She smiled winningly. 'How much would I get for that, do you think?'

But before he could reply a hand viciously gripped her shoulder from behind and spun her around. She just had time to see it was a beautiful woman when her face stung from a slap delivered by that same lady.

'What do you think you're playing at, you stinking cow?!' the woman spat into Belinda's face, confusing her terribly. Belinda was so shocked she could only stammer, 'I – I – just wanted to earn some money—!'

'Yeah, I heard you trying to poach one of our boys!' she shouted, causing a hush to fall on the nearest tables whose occupants looked on with amusement. Belinda now saw that the woman was not as beautiful as she had appeared. Beneath her fine hairstyle and her glamorous clothing and make-up she had a very harsh and world-worn face.

Belinda was terrified. 'I... I'm terribly sorry. I meant no harm.' In fact she still didn't know what she had done wrong.

The sour witch jabbed a long painted fingernail into Belinda's right nipple to emphasise each of her hissed words. 'Nobody – works – this – bar – without – going

100

'– through – me—'

Poor bewildered Belinda tried to back away from the brutal finger, but the bulk of the big man blocked her retreat.

'You better come with me,' decided the witch. 'My husband will need to deal with this.' So saying she grabbed Belinda painfully by the arm, propelled the terrified girl through the jeering crowds, and into an office at the far end of the bar.

It was a fair-sized room, furnished with a large leather-topped desk and a variety of comfortable-looking chairs. The floor was carpeted in deep colours and there were red velvet curtains at the window. Belinda's nose wrinkled at the pervading smell of stale sweat that clung to the air.

A man was seated at the desk, and he looked up as his wife pushed Belinda into the room. He was an unpleasant-looking type; dark and rat-faced with a thin black moustache and slicked-back hair parted in the middle. Belinda also noticed his attempt at a bow tie. She thought it looked more like a badly knotted bootlace than a tie. His sharp little eyes lit up as he took in Belinda's beauty and fullness of figure.

'Well, well, well,' he said as she squirmed under his lecherous gaze. 'What have we here then?'

'Caught this little heifer trying a mite of freelancing up at the bar, Charlie,' said the woman, shaking Belinda by her upper arm.

'Good for you, Ruth dearest,' he said with a sickly smile without taking his eyes from the exceedingly promising Belinda. 'What do you think you were up to, girl?' he snapped suddenly. The smile was gone.

'I just needed to earn a little money,' sobbed Belinda.

'Don't give us that little-miss-innocent shit!'

bellowed Ruth. She reached around Belinda and cupped and lifted her soft breasts. Belinda gasped at the disgraceful liberty, but said nothing. 'She's stood there talking to Cy No-Nose and she's wiggling these at him and telling him she could play a fine tune for him if the price was right,' sneered Ruth.

Belinda was relieved to hear the horrible Charlie chuckle at that.

'Well,' he said, 'not only have you got the right sort of pretty face,' his beady eyes roamed to her proffered breasts and he licked his thin moustache, 'but sounds like you got experience and wit as well. You could be what we're looking for, eh, wife?'

Ruth squeezed her back against her own generous bosom. 'I think she might fit in,' she sniggered.

Belinda's heart leapt.

'Course, we'll have to deal with her in the usual way for trying to steal our clients,' continued Charlie.

'But I wasn't—' Belinda started to protest.

'And for lying as well,' added Ruth, though she sounded more pleased than annoyed.

Belinda decided to shut up.

'Girl like you can make a lot of money here, so long as you go through the right channels,' said Charlie, standing up. 'We got lots of gentlemen with spare money want to pay well for odd jobs. Know what I mean?'

Belinda nodded brightly. This was more like it. Especially as Ruth had now released her breasts from the crushing grip.

'But she's got to take a beating for her dishonest trading, hasn't she Charlie?' said Ruth, with a whining hint of concern in her voice.

'What's your name, girl,' asked Charlie casually.

'Belinda, sir,' she answered meekly.

'Very well, Belinda, we'll find you the clients and we'll pay you well. But only if you accept your punishment. You deserve it and it'll show us what you're worth.'

Belinda was too desperate for the chance to earn a living to raise any objection. She nodded. She was ready for whatever they were intending to do... But then their demeanour changed, and a sinister chill ran up her spine.

'Just come over here, darling,' whispered Ruth into her ear as she guided her gently towards the desk.

As Belinda's thighs pressed against the mahogany edge Charlie smiled politely and, opening a drawer, took out a thick polished cane whose segments were clearly divided by the raised rings evenly spaced along its length. It looked heavy and Belinda felt the familiar tightening of the skin on her bottom. For all her unfortunate experience, she had never decided which was worst – thin and whippy or thick and weighty.

Charlie leered almost apologetically at Belinda and whipped the cane onto the leather back of his chair. The crack nearly made her leap out of her skin and left her visibly trembling.

Charlie moved around the desk and stood beside her. 'Sorry,' he whispered, and pressing on the small of her back, he bent her over the desk. The heady aroma of old leather filled her nostrils as she felt Ruth's hands ghost their way up her legs from ankle to thigh, before folding her dress up onto her back. She felt a cold draught on her exposed buttocks, which was quickly replaced by a warm one as lips caressed their silkiness. She knew it was Ruth, because Charlie was standing with his solid erection pressing through his trousers against her hip. Belinda squealed softly with surprise as Ruth licked her bottom. Charlie stroked her

103

hair almost tenderly and traced the tip of the cane around her slightly parted lips. Belinda squealed again as the rude tongue wormed its way between her buttocks. The feeling was not at all unpleasant, but she could have died when the persistent intruder pressed against her most private entrance, and then popped just inside. As she opened her mouth to protest the cane slipped in and silenced her. She gradually melted as the clever tongue wriggled and teased in her rear passage, and when a finger eased between her thighs and caressed her wet labia her legs buckled and she draped panting and helpless on top of the desk. As she closed her eyes and drifted towards a wonderful orgasm the expert digits disappeared, and she was left dismayed and empty. How could this man and wife be so cruel?

'She'll do,' she heard Ruth's assessment through clouds of swirling confusion. Hands rolled her onto her back, and she peered up at the couple through lowered lashes. Charlie laid the cane on the desk and helped his wife remove her dress. In moments Ruth wore only a tight corset that threatened to spill her voluminous bosom, and a pair of white knee-length drawers. She climbed onto the desk and knelt astride Belinda's waist. Her hands gently stroked along the prostrate girl's enticing curves, and then with another menacing change of mood she gripped her bodice and ripped it open. Belinda's gorgeous breasts spilled out, and both husband and wife exhaled with admiration and desire.

'Wonderful!' Ruth panted for them both.

Belinda, not daring to provoke this unpredictable couple, lay quiet and still as Ruth squirmed up her body until she sat heavily on her naked breasts. Her arms were trapped uselessly by Ruth's legs. Belinda didn't know what to expect next from the woman who knelt gazing down at her, and then she felt with embarrassment Charlie stroking her flat stomach and soft thatch.

'Right, Charlie,' whispered Ruth, 'you may begin…'

Belinda howled at the terrible shock of the cane lashing across her thighs. She begged for mercy with tear-filled eyes, but the kneeling woman merely smiled down at her enigmatically. She felt Charlie adjust her legs a little wider, and then the cane struck repeatedly.

As her husband set about those exquisitely formed limbs, Ruth inched her hips forward and smothered the girl's pleas beneath her cotton underwear. Her knuckles nudged those hot, tearstained cheeks as she opened the ingenious gusset and settled her inflamed sex over the girl's lovely mouth. She didn't need to utter instructions, because every time the cane whooshed and slashed the frantic mouth twitched and kissed and licked. It wasn't the most refined performance of cunnilingus she had ever experienced, but it was one of the most enjoyable.

Belinda lost count of the blows, but there must have been around thirty delivered before Ruth shrieked and ground herself harder against her abused mouth, and slumped panting and moaning on top of her. She hoped the couple were finished, but was quickly disappointed.

Ruth relaxed and squirmed against Belinda until their lips met. She kissed her new toy gently, and manoeuvred her slightly on the desk. Belinda felt something press persistently into her cheek. She opened her eyes, fearing the worst. Her head was close to the edge of the desk, and Charlie had his penis in his fist and was masturbating silently but determinedly against her flushed face. Belinda whimpered as Ruth eased her head to the side and used her fingers to peel her moist lips apart. She took a deep breath and watched the shiny plum move closer. A little liquid dribbled from the tip as she felt it stretch her lips even wider and then slide beyond her teeth and deep into her vulnerable mouth. She followed Ruth's whispered instructions and sucked as best she could. She could taste his saltiness. Fingers pinched and coaxed her nipples. Others stroked her hair. Heavy balls swung against her chin, and she was engulfed by his humid groin and Ruth's feverish lips kissing her perspiring face. The thick shaft grew ever more rigid and throbbed urgently against the back of her throat. Belinda knew he was close, and prepared to swallow what promised to be a copious eruption. He grunted and stiffened. Ruth hissed triumphantly. Belinda braced herself – but he suddenly withdrew and splattered his seed onto her trembling breasts. Ruth hastily sucked greedily on Belinda's erect nipples and massaged her husband's ejaculation into the soft mounds of flesh. Charlie fell upon the shell-shocked girl, and the husband and wife each devoured a breast as though she was a sumptuous feast and they were near starvation. Belinda closed her eyes and readied herself for whatever else they chose to do to her. But gradually their fervour seemed to wane, and after a short while their attentions ceased altogether. Ruth put her dress back on and helped Belinda stand and straighten her own clothing, and Charlie resumed his place behind the desk. Belinda wondered why they had not gone further, and if pressed would have had to admit to being just a little disappointed.

'She'll do,' Ruth confirmed again, the passion still evident in her voice.

Charlie nodded. 'Next time, Belinda,' he said

huskily whilst fastening his trousers, 'we'll have more time, and then we'll have some *real* fun.'

After that introductory session Belinda was whisked away by a friendlier Ruth to a nearby lodging house for the night. She was excited at Ruth's having given her three nearly new gowns and some exotic underwear, and luxuriated in a hot bath whilst the kindly but solemn landlady poured water over her and helped her rub heavenly soap into every nook of her body. Belinda got the distinct impression that the landlady was thoroughly enjoying this task, but was beyond caring about such minor matters. She had been told to report back to the saloon – the Crazy Horn – early the next evening when there would be some rewarding work awaiting.

When she duly arrived at the appointed hour she was excited and happy, and this, together with her revealingly low-cut red velvet gown and her hair arranged in dangling ringlets, was enough to silence the bedlam of the bar when she walked in. Blushing radiantly at the cacophony of whistles and lewd remarks that broke the stunned silence, she was immediately rescued by Ruth, who, after complimenting her beauty most highly, took her by the arm and led her to a table in a corner.

A man was sitting there and he rose to greet her with great courtesy.

'Sheriff,' cooed Ruth with a sweetness that didn't really suit her, 'this is Belinda. Ain't she something?' Turning to Belinda she said, 'Belinda, darling, this is our very own Sheriff, Sheriff Hanglin. He gets well paid to protect this town and he's a generous man to those he takes a shine to.' With that she winked at the Sheriff, gave Belinda an embarrassing pat on her backside, and flounced away.

The Sheriff was a sinister figure. Dressed in a black suit and wide-brimmed hat, his high-cheekboned face was spattered with deep pock marks below his cold eyes. His black moustache was long and drooped down below his jaw on either side of thin lips. Belinda cautiously eyed his silver star marked *Sheriff*, and his belt full of bullets and the gun on each hip. He said nothing, but simply stared at her with narrow eyes that gave little away.

Belinda was just wondering whether to speak, or sit, or something, when he spoke.

'You ready to get to work, girl?' he asked in a quiet, metallic voice that sent a small shiver down her spine.

'Oh... yes, sir,' she replied more brightly than she felt. 'What sort of a task did you have in mind?'

'Well, how's about you giving my riding equipment a real good polish?'

'Oh, I'm very good at that!' she exclaimed happily. 'I used to love doing my father's and brother's...' her voice trailed off as she remembered happier days.

The Sheriff chuckled grimly. 'Sounds like my kind of girl. Let's get, then.'

'What, now?' said Belinda. 'I mean, I'm not really dressed for that sort of thing.'

The Sheriff chuckled again. 'You're dressed just fine,' he said, picking up his riding crop from the table. 'Come on.'

Belinda followed him across the bar, noting how each group of drunks fell silent as he passed. To her surprise, instead of heading for the main door, he led her up the stairs to the first floor landing. She followed him into a room and he closed the door behind her. It was small, smelly, and sparsely furnished with just an upright chair, a small cupboard, and a bed, all of which were revealed when he struck a match and lit the

108

paraffin lamp.

From the cupboard he took a silver canister and removed the lid. He handed it to Belinda, who looked a little puzzled.

'Saddle soap,' he said easily.

'Oh, dubbin!' she cried with happy recognition. She dipped her fingers into the slippery white wax and felt it ooze between them. 'Right-oh,' she said, feeling a little happier now, 'if you'll just show me your riding equipment I'll get started.'

She knew she should have know better, and cursed her naivety when he patted the front of his trousers, revealing the shape of a very large erection. Her spirits plummeted again as she stood there, red-faced, and watched him casually undo his trousers and pull out an exceptionally large penis. He stared at her and arrogantly stroked it a few times.

'Come here,' he ordered.

With a growing feeling of misery and disillusionment, Belinda obeyed. He was the sort that few would defy.

As she stood in front of him, feeling his erection pulsating against her belly through the gown, she mustered one last stand of defiance.

'I'm sorry,' she said with a coolness she didn't really feel, 'but I must ask you to put that away and show me your riding equipment, or I shall be forced to call the management.'

That was the funniest, if not the only funny thing, he had ever heard, judging by the roar of laughter that escaped his wooden face. But as quickly as it came the mirth was gone. He gripped her delicate hand, pressed it to the offending erection, and squeezed her cool fingers around its considerable girth.

'This,' he said in a level tone, 'is my riding

equipment. It's what I use for riding pretty girls like you. Now, you want to earn some good money or not?'

Belinda did not simply *want* to earn some good money, she simply *had* to. She wrestled with her conscience – but only very briefly. Once she'd made enough money to get out of that town she would never ever do such things again – she promised herself.

Too choked with shame and other negative emotions, she could not bring herself to admit defeat by saying yes, but signalled her servility by humbly lowering her gaze and giving his powerful column one long slow stroke.

'Good girl,' he said with an air that suggested he expected nothing less. 'The better you perform, the quicker you get rich,' he chuckled unnecessarily. 'Now, let's get on without any further nonsense, shall we?' With that he guided her hand into the gaping shadows of his trousers and made her cup his balls. They were large and heavy, and Belinda dreaded to think how much they contained. As she tentatively explored them his erection throbbed along her forearm like a sleeping serpent. The skin on the huge purple helmet was stretched taut and shone like polished marble, and he opened her free hand and placed it in the damp palm as though giving her a present. He coolly eyed her flushed face and nervously swelling breasts as he removed his gun belt and dropped his trousers. He then removed his jacket and shirt, and stood before her in only his hat and boots.

'Come on, you've had your fun,' he said. 'Now get polishing.'

His requirements were obvious – even to Belinda – so she picked up the tin of saddle soap, scooped out a thick dollop, and coated it liberally onto his waiting penis. He grunted a little and his greased stalk pulsed appreciatively as she worked, rubbing her fist up and down and all around. She became absorbed in her task and, as was her nature, toiled to the best of her ability. The rearing stalk became smoother and shinier as more and more of the glutinous stuff was worked into it, and he was clearly becoming more and more aroused. At last the canister was empty, and the Sheriff's erection looked and felt like a large candle.

Belinda looked up at him, and thought for a split second she detected just the slightest flicker of emotion in his stony black eyes. She allowed him to take the empty canister from her and place it on the chair, and then stood stoically as he grasped her breasts and mauled them through the soft velvet dress. There was no finesse about the man, and Belinda knew he was only intent on pleasing himself.

'Looks to me like you done a good job there.' His broad chest rose and fell heavily before he continued. 'Guess I should take it for a ride and try it out... Get your dress off, and kneel by the bed.'

He watched without expression as the beauty stripped to her corset, drawers, and stockings, and then obediently knelt like a child saying her bedtime prayers. Her protests were without conviction or hope as he forced her onto all fours and positioned her cheek on the mattress so she wouldn't move forward.

Her morals had been temporarily neutralised by her need to earn money in a good cause, which made it easier for her to feel a hint of pleasure as she felt him kneel behind her, tug down her drawers, and rest that rather fine specimen between her buttocks.

Sheriff Hanglin began to move his slick member up and down, and each stroke brought its massive head lower and lower until it was bumping against her pudenda. He shuffled nearer so his groin pressed against her bottom, forcing her face into the deep mattress and his penis firmly against her clitoris. Belinda could not suppress the surge of excitement at the intimate caress.

Then with the slightest thrust he was inside her, and her mouth gaped in unison with his long slow entry. Eventually he was fully embedded, and Belinda bit the musty bedspread to smother her scream of joy.

But he did not move once he was in. He waited a few seconds and then said, 'Now then young lady, gallop!'

Since Belinda was in no position to move she did nothing. She heard him grunt and then there was a movement and an agonising crack as his riding crop struck the side of her thigh. She screamed and jumped.

'That's better!' he rasped as her vagina milked his penis. 'Now gallop!'

Still Belinda could not move significantly. Her face and shoulders were squashed into the bed and his weight pressed down on her. But she knew the whip would not be long in cutting her flesh again if she did not please him, so she twisted and ground her bottom back against his solid and unmoving belly. The whip clattered to the floor and he reached beneath her and weighed her breasts in one hand and stroked her clitoris with the other. Belinda rolled her head, and he responded to her sensual gyrations by thrusting into her with increasing urgency. Fingers dug into her hips and the room was filled with the sound of his groin slapping against her buttocks. As the beautiful orgasm quickly washed through her straining and perspiring body Sheriff Hanglin roared and erupted copiously. Belinda stiffened as he filled her again and again, and then slowly relaxed into the bed as she felt his intensity lessen and his wet and deflating penis slip away.

He gave her a one dollar banknote. She was astonished to realise that up to now she had had no contact with American money. 'What's this?' she asked as they dressed.

'It's a dollar,' he snapped. 'What do you think it is?'

'Yes, but what's it worth?'

'It's worth a dollar,' he sneered sarcastically. 'That's what it's worth.'

'No, I mean what's it worth in pounds, or shillings?'

'How the hell should I know?' He started angrily towards the door, but as he opened it he stopped, thought, and looked back. 'Let's just say that if you had about fifty of them you could buy a halfway decent horse.'

As Belinda descended the stairs, braving the smugly knowing grins of the clientele looking up at her, and the less than friendly looks of the ladies who worked there, Belinda saw the Sheriff go over to Ruth and Charlie and give them a monetary note. Quickly passing close behind out of curiosity, Belinda heard the Sheriff say, 'Ten dollars, that right?'

'That's right, Sheriff. You give her a tip?'

The Sheriff grinned. 'I give her two tips. The tip of my dick and a dollar for herself.' He sniggered at his very clever joke and the couple laughed heartily, although they didn't seem too sure why.

Belinda approached Ruth and Charlie after the satisfied Sheriff had left them.

'Well, I did it,' she said, pleased with herself for having the courage to do a job properly, no matter how distasteful it might be. 'When do I get paid?' she enquired pleasantly.

Charlie's eyes narrowed, and the men around them

113

fell silent. 'Get paid?' he echoed. 'I thought the Sheriff gave you a dollar?'

'Well, yes, but that was just a tip. He gave you ten dollars. Surely a big part of that must be mine? I earned it after all.'

Charlie and Ruth looked around uneasily at the listening men. 'Sure honey,' said Ruth. 'But we don't spoil the fun by talking cash in front of the customers. When the evening's done come and see us and we'll settle up. How's that?'

'Oh, all right then,' said Belinda happily and, as bidden by Ruth, went to the bar and ordered herself a free drink.

By the time the bar closed at three o'clock in the morning, Ruth and Charlie had found Belinda four more clients, each with unusual requirements. There had been a coarsely unshaven old cowhand who stank of stale urine and whose barbed wire whiskers had scraped her nipples as he masturbated against her naked body. A fat youth, whose wide girth she had to sit astride while they made love, and two others who were pretty unforgettable – and their sexual prowess even more unforgettable. But they had all given her a dollar, making a total of five for the evening, and she still had her wages to collect from Charlie and Ruth. Gosh, at that rate she only had to put up with this awful life for a few days more and she could then buy a decent horse and afford to travel to California in style.

She had to wait alone in the dimmed and eerily silent bar for her employers to finish cashing up in the office, and she amused herself by sitting on a tiny stool and playing the piano, until she was startled by Charlie's voice right behind her.

'After all we done for you.'

Startled Belinda whirled around. 'I beg your pardon?'

'Who the fuck you think you are trying to make a show of us in front of our customers?' he snarled.

'But… I don't understand. The men gave you ten dollars—'

'We don't care if they give us a hundred dollars!' snapped Ruth. 'As long as you got your dollar that's all you got to worry about. Normal girls work hard all week for a dollar, so shut your crap!'

'I—'

'You're an ungrateful little sow, ain't you?' sneered Charlie. 'We fix you up with a good job off the street, give you food, lodging, clothes, premises to work in, find you the customers… and what? You start screaming for more, more, more.'

'I – I'm sorry…' stammered Belinda. 'I didn't think I was…'

'I say kick her out now, Charlie,' said Ruth. 'I reckon she's going to be more trouble than she's worth. None of the other girls like her anyhow.'

Belinda was more disturbed by that than anything. She'd hardly had time to say hello to the others, and was dismayed to hear that they had taken an instant dislike to her. 'No – please. I won't be any trouble.'

'Ah, they're just jealous because she's got what it takes for the big money,' Charlie said to his wife. Turning again to Belinda he added, 'They'd kill for the chance to earn a dollar a trick, you unappreciative little bitch.'

Belinda hung her head and wished she could simply vanish.

'If she wants to stay here she's going to have to accept her correction, Charlie.'

'Yep.'

Belinda sighed sadly. 'Do I have to? I promise not to embarrass you again in front of the customers.'

'Have to? Don't have to do nothing,' snapped Ruth. 'You come in here a free bird, you can just up and get out a free bird, too. You wanna stay though, you get a whupping.'

Belinda had no choice but to stay in their employ; she still desperately needed the money. She reluctantly nodded her acceptance of the correction, and without even being asked, in fact almost unaware of what she was doing, she rose from the piano stool and undressed. She had to wait then while Ruth went to the office and came back holding some small items of clothing, as well as a pair of wooden-backed clothes brushes. Belinda put one foot at a time on the stool and rolled up the black stockings given her by Ruth – much to Charlie's obvious approval – and then tied a purple velvet bow around her slender throat. Between the bow and the stocking-tops she was gloriously naked.

She was ordered to bend and place her hands on the stool. When she was positioned just so, the spiteful couple set about her beautiful bottom with the clothes brushes. The punishment was extremely vigorous, and the dazed girl struggled to maintain her balance. On one occasion she rocked forward and the piano emitted a macabre and haunting chord as the keyboard prevented her from toppling to the floor. The punishment continued until her raised bottom glowed red, and then she was left sniffling in the darkness as the couple doused the few remaining lights and retired, giggling, to their quarters.

116

Chapter Seven

Belinda worked at the Crazy Horn every night for almost six weeks, and saved over a hundred dollars, enough to buy a horse and provisions to get her all the way to her uncle's place in a matter of weeks.

She had been able to save every penny she had earned, depositing it in the local bank, because all of her food, lodging and drinks were provided free with her job. However, well paid as the work was, she could not wait to get away from it and be done with that sort of life forever.

She had had a great variety of clients over those few weeks, all of them interested in variations on the same sort of theme, which meant beating Belinda. Only one stood out for his difference. A boy of no more than seventeen. He had undressed to reveal her first ever sight of a pair of long johns. The tight fit meant that his penis, though not erect, was clearly outlined through the cotton.

The boy had shocked Belinda by telling her that he wanted her to cane him. Apparently he had been used to this sort of treatment all his life and found it very sexy when dispensed by a woman. Belinda had tried to comply, but she was not accustomed to it, especially in cold blood, and she could not bring herself to cane him with any force. The boy had complained to Ruth, who had come up to the room, shouted at Belinda, and taken over quite happily. She had undone the back flap so that his bottom was revealed, framed in the square opening, and had then undone his fly buttons and pulled out his cock. Belinda had simply to kneel and suck the boy whilst Ruth threw herself fully into caning his exposed backside. Ruth had been delighted, because as she said, it wasn't often she had the chance to chastise a man. Belinda had found no trouble in sucking him, not after all her experiences, and she was intrigued at the way his cock kept lurching and hardening in her mouth with each stroke of the cane until he clutched her head tightly and made her swallow his youthful ejaculation.

Belinda also learnt other things during her stay. The town was called Golden Seat and was about fifty miles west of a larger town called Denver. Golden Seat, it transpired, was in fact a private estate owned by three rich and respectable women called the Spinsters Union. They had bought the land in the middle of nowhere and had built the town, equipping it and populating it with trades people. Nobody knew their reasons for doing this, but presumably they made a living from the rents they charged. As it was a private estate, they were also responsible for law and order. They had hired Sheriff Hanglin and left it to him to deal with the male lawbreakers, but they apparently insisted on taking charge of administering various degrees of corporal punishment to any female wrongdoers that he brought before them. Belinda was surprised – in view of her own sad background – to hear that the punishment was perfectly straight and involved no sex. In fact she had felt embarrassed at having expressed such a thought, and was told very sharply that the Spinsters Union could not and would not do any wrong.

The person who corrected her was Jennifer, the only one of the Crazy Horn girls who had been at all friendly to Belinda. Jennifer said that was because the others were jealous and resentful of Belinda's ability to take so many beatings and earn double the money.

Belinda and Jennifer shared the same room, indeed the same bed, at the lodging house, and Belinda was so touched by Jennifer's kindness – the only kindness she could recall having received in America – that she had not minded when Jennifer touched and stroked her as they chatted in bed. Indeed, she found Jennifer's fingers bringing her to orgasm somehow wholesome compared with the viciousness to which she was used. She also enjoyed reciprocating, but always at Jennifer's bidding, and she always tried to forget that she had done such a thing when she awoke the next morning. She had told Jennifer the full tragedy of her landing in Virginia.

Belinda was dismayed to learn one night that her journey so far had been a 'doddle' compared to what lay ahead. The Sheriff had taken great delight in advising her of this fact whilst having a drink at the bar.

'What you've done is like a stroll in a country park compared to what lies ahead,' he said, casually mauling her breasts as he spoke. 'Those black shadows you see on the horizon, them's the Rocky Mountains, the wildest most murderous crossing in the world, I reckon. And if you survive them, well you've still got Death Valley to get through, so I guess you ain't got no chance.'

Daunted but still determined, Belinda swore to herself that she would just have to get across somehow. It was either that or stay in Golden Seat, and that was not an option for which she cared.

Belinda also knew where she was heading now. She had come a long way too far north, but the town she wanted was now directly southwest of where she was, and The Angels turned out to be simply called Los Angeles.

119

Then things went savagely wrong. Belinda had just finished with her last client, not just of the evening, but forever. Sitting on the edge of the bed, eagerly contemplating her departure from Golden Seat, she was still dressed in the outfit her last client had insisted she wear; a short soft leather skirt, a diaphanous white blouse, the tiniest pair of white cotton drawers, and a pair of high-heeled boots. There was a sharp knock at the door. She groaned and called out that she was finished for the night.

'Open the door. It's the Sheriff.'

'I'm sorry, Sheriff,' she called. 'I can't take any more tonight.' Or ever again, she thought to herself.

There was a splinter and a crunch and the door flew open under the impact of the Sheriff's boot. He strode into the room with gun in hand as Belinda hastily rose and backed away. She stared at him in terror; something was seriously amiss.

'Belinda Hopeworth, I do hereby arrest you for the murder and robbery of one William Wandle at Norfolk, Virginia, on a date as yet unspecified. You will come with me.'

Despite her shrieks of innocence he gripped Belinda by the arm and dragged her downstairs, out into the street and down to his office. He threw her into a cell, formed by barring off one end of the office, and told her that news of the warrant for her arrest had just reached Golden Seat.

With heart pounding Belinda asked what was going to happen. He said she would be transported back to Norfolk to stand trial before being hanged. Belinda felt faint and nauseous, and slumped down on the bare bench as he left her in the dark.

A little later he returned and lit the oil lamps.

'Good news,' he said with a slimy smile. 'Spinsters

120

Union says they can't spare me to take you all the way to Norfolk, and there's no one else they can trust…'

Belinda relaxed – just a little.

'They also says that being a lady you ought to be whipped and not hanged. Up to you – yes or no?'

'But I've done nothing wrong!' she protested.

'Yes or no?' he repeated.

Belinda did not hesitate further. 'Well yes, of course!' she nodded earnestly. 'I'll do anything… just please don't hang me!'

'Good. Spinsters Union don't believe in hanging. You let them deal with you in their own way and you can live.' He chuckled. 'Even if you don't much feel like it afterwards.'

Sheriff Hanglin bundled Belinda through the dark and deserted main street at gunpoint until they reached the smarter part of town where the white villas were. He led her to the large courthouse, opened the door and pushed her inside.

Belinda looked around timidly. At the end of the stark room, on a raised dais, sat three precisely dressed women behind a wide and highly polished desk.

'Approach the bench,' the Sheriff instructed tersely and guided her forward and up the steps of the dais.

'Meet the Spinsters Union,' he said and introduced each lady in turn. The one in the middle was quite elderly, stout, and had the air of a strict headmistress. She was Miss Rothschild. To her left sat an extremely attractive women. Tall and well built, she fixed a contemptuous stare on Belinda. Her glorious red hair contrasted vividly with her green gown. Her name was Miss Ladyfield. To the right of Miss Rothschild sat a scrawny middle-aged woman with a mad glint in her eyes. 'Miss Katz,' the Sheriff concluded the introductions, and then withdrew to leave Belinda to face the formidable tribunal. She noticed his demeanour was much more respectful than usual.

The ladies studied Belinda with little emotion.

'You have agreed to be dealt with by us?' Miss Rothschild broke the uneasy silence.

'I have,' Belinda nodded, noting that her Scottish accent suitably complemented her stern appearance. 'But I have to tell you that I am totally innocent of any charges set against me—'

'Silence!' snapped Miss Rothschild. 'You disrespectful delinquent! Is it not enough that we have to convene this session at such an ungodly hour, without having to suffer your impertinence?'

Miss Ladyfield and Miss Katz tutted and shook their heads with disapproval.

'I feel we should instigate proceedings without further ado,' said the haughty Miss Ladyfield without interrupting her inspection of Belinda's lovely form.

'I have to agree, Elizabeth,' concurred Miss Katz solemnly. 'It seems the reprobate is in urgent need of discipline.'

'Quite,' nodded Miss Rothschild. 'Sheriff, would you kindly mind the door for us. We do not wish to be disturbed.'

'Ma'am,' he touched the rim of his hat.

'You may watch,' she added, 'but remain alert.'

'Yes ma'am.'

His humility astonished Belinda, and increased her wariness of the three women. Were they insane?

Miss Katz rose and moved behind Belinda. 'Look to the front,' she ordered calmly.

Belinda focused her attention on Miss Rothschild as icy fingers slid up under the leather skirt and stroked her smooth thighs until they found the round contours of her bottom. They prodded and probed between her

122

legs, nudged them slightly wider apart, and then rubbed her sex-lips through the crisp cotton panties. Afraid to move away she wriggled slightly to show her dislike for such attention. But this was misinterpreted.

'Oh yes, you like it,' cooed Miss Katz, pressing the cotton against her clitoris.

'An excellent response,' adjudged Miss Rothschild.

'She is a highly sensitive young lady,' confirmed Miss Katz, her fingers and the undergarment sinking deeper into Belinda's moist tunnel.

Miss Ladyfield rose and joined her colleague. Just as Belinda felt her traitorous insides beginning to melt the fingers disappeared. She gasped softly. Miss Katz moved to her front, studying her slick fingertips with great interest, and then traced them across Belinda's lips. When Belinda pulled away the nasty woman forced them roughly into her mouth and held them there. 'You dirty young lady!' she hissed. 'Give her the cane!'

Belinda stiffened, but Miss Ladyfield held her firmly.

'No Kitty, not the cane,' answered Miss Rothschild pensively. 'I think the tawse to begin with,' she decided with a smile.

'Oh yes!' enthused Miss Ladyfield. Without being asked she went to a cupboard and returned with a strap. She held the implement before Belinda. 'Have you ever seen a tawse before?' she inquired, her eyes afire.

'I have,' muttered Belinda shamefully.

'This is to our own design,' said Miss Rothschild proudly.

Miss Ladyfield turned the strap over and showed Belinda that each separate part of the tawse had a small weight sewn onto it. 'The weights serve to increase the momentum with the minimum of effort,' she explained, 'but we have made them unequal, so that each half travels at a different speed and one arrives just after the other, giving a double blow. Clever?'

Belinda nodded instinctively.

'Let us begin,' said the stern Miss Rothschild.

Belinda obeyed the instruction to place her hands on her head, and then watched without complaint as Miss Katz knelt, lifted the hem of the leather skirt, and nuzzled her face against her soft mound through the damp white drawers. The elegant Miss Ladyfield, with tawse in hand, cupped Belinda's vulnerable breasts with delicate fingers and kissed her throat. Miss Rothschild busied herself with a full-length mirror, positioned it in front of the gently panting and squirming threesome, and then resumed her seat. Belinda gazed through misty eyes at the reflected scene; her hands on her head, Miss Ladyfield squeezing her breasts and flicking her erect nipples through the blouse, and the head of Miss Katz undulating gently beneath the skirt.

After a few minutes, and to Belinda's secret disappointment, Miss Ladyfield moved back a step and lifted the short skirt. Belinda held her breath. Miss Katz slurped quietly. Miss Rothschild nodded, and there was a severe double crack. Belinda jerked and squealed as the two halves of leather bit the backs of her thighs a split second apart.

'Good shot, Elizabeth,' encouraged Miss Rothschild. 'Perhaps a little harder next time?'

Elizabeth Ladyfield, closely studying Belinda's face in the mirror, flicked her wrist once more. Belinda shrieked as the double sting struck again – and again, and then again. The clever mouth between her thighs worked enthusiastically. Fingers moved the gusset of her drawers aside, and a tongue wormed insistently into her hot tunnel. Belinda jerked forward at each swipe of the leather, and the tongue stabbed deeper each time. She moaned and her legs trembled, and just as she threatened to orgasm over the industrious mouth of Miss Katz the beating ceased. The tawse fell to the floor and Belinda was shocked as Miss Ladyfield crushed her in a powerful embrace and kissed her deeply and passionately. Belinda trembled with mounting excitement, and could not prevent herself from groaning into the attractive lady's mouth.

'Elizabeth... Kitty...' Miss Rothschild's severe voice interrupted the sweet slurping and panting of the three females. 'That's enough of that for now.'

Miss Ladyfield broke away from the kiss while Miss Katz stood, patted her hair into place, and regained her composure. Both ladies were clearly highly aroused. Belinda was in a daze. She remained with her hands on her head and breasts heaving as Miss Rothschild studied her body relentlessly.

'You really are quite adorable, my dear,' she said evenly, and then nodded to her two colleagues.

Belinda allowed them to position her over the bench without a sound of protest; she knew it would be useless. Miss Rothschild gripped her wrists and held them firmly so she could not move or protect herself. 'I think we are ready for the cane,' she announced.

Belinda watched over her shoulder as Miss Ladyfield went to the same cupboard and returned with two canes. She disappeared from her line of vision, and then she felt cold fingers raise the leather skirt and tug the drawers down to her knees.

'You will each administer six strokes,' Miss Rothschild instructed, and then looked at Belinda.

125

'And you will take your punishment bravely. Do you understand?'

Belinda nodded, closed her eyes, and waited.

A hand gently smoothed her exposed buttocks... There was a sudden swish and fire licked across Belinda's bottom. She jerked on the polished bench, but Miss Rothschild held her firm with surprising ease. A second swish quickly followed and Belinda writhed again. Her wrists were clamped in one hand and a second soothed her hair as Miss Rothschild whispered encouragement to her. The punishment continued remorselessly as Belinda bit her lip and sobbed quietly; she was determined not to cry for mercy.

Eventually the unjust beating was over. The two canes were placed carefully on the bench, and then fingers dipped into her soaking vagina. Belinda had not the inclination or ability to resist, and quickly she was brought to a shuddering orgasm on the bench while Miss Rothschild gently soothed and stroked her hair.

Her wrists were released and she stood stiffly, sniffling and wiping her wet eyes on her sleeves. The leather skirt swayed not unpleasantly against her sore bottom.

'You have done very well, my dear,' said Miss Rothschild. 'You have accepted your punishment with admirable dignity.'

It was over. She was free. She would gather her money, buy a horse, and head for the Rockies.

'However,' continued Miss Rothschild, the smile leaving her icy eyes, 'you are clearly guilty of murder.'

'No!'

'We don't believe in hanging,' the brutal woman ignored the interruption. 'You will therefore spend twenty years in the special dungeon below the

Sheriff's office, with only him – and sometimes us – as
visitors... Sheriff!'

Chapter Eight

Hanglin pushed Belinda through the dark and empty streets in a state of acute excitement. He walked close behind the stunned girl, prodding his erection against her at every step. Familiar as she was with his 'riding equipment', she had never known it in such a state of arousal. As he rushed her towards the cell he was panting in a way that would have worried the town doctor.

'Belinda,' he rasped in her ear, 'you should have seen it all from where I was watching. You were terrific. Let's get back to the cell!'

All Belinda could think about was spending her whole life over again locked up for a crime she did not commit. This could not be happening to her. She tried to think constructively but her mind was in a spin, and having the Sheriff jabbing and pinching her like an annoying schoolboy did not help.

'I've never felt so fucking randy, Belinda,' he wheezed as he manhandled her into the cell. 'I'm so worked up by watching you tonight! Belinda, I want you to do something to me I've always dreamt of but couldn't risk the scandal. I trust you, and with you going to be shut off from the world for such a long time...'

Belinda stared at him in abject misery. What devious fantasy had he in mind? Apparently nothing that new, she sighed, as he unbuckled his belt and pulled it from his trouser loops.

Clearly trembling and sweating profusely he took his handcuffs. Belinda stared at them miserably. She knew what was coming. But then he clipped one cuff around his right wrist and offered the other to her. 'Belinda… please. You've just got to do it. I've been going crazy since I first saw you. I knew you were the one to fulfil my dream.'

Belinda gawped in disbelief. 'You – you mean you want me to…?'

'You must! Handcuff me to the bars and beat me!'

The sweat was bursting out on his brow and staining his shirt beneath his arms. Before Belinda could gather her thoughts he removed his gun belt and dropped his trousers. His erection was larger and throbbed more fiercely than she had ever seen before. Half expecting a sudden mood swing she cautiously took the offered cuff, threaded it around one of the bars of the cell, locked it onto his other wrist, and stepped back.

He was tethered – and could not escape! She must be dreaming. Normally he would have been right to trust her – she was a very trustworthy young lady – but present circumstances were somewhat extreme. She checked the metal bonds. He really was unable to touch or pursue her. This was all too difficult to believe.

'Please Belinda!' he croaked.

Her immediate instinct was to flee, but she was cautious. 'Why should I do any more to please you? Haven't you taken enough pleasure from me since I came to this loathsome place?'

'Please! Now's your chance for revenge! Use your anger and beat me. I deserve it!'

Belinda glanced surreptitiously at his angry erection spearing up from his groin. It was truly impressive and she felt her stomach tighten at the sight. She slowly reached out, curled her fingers around its length, and firmly stroked back and forth. 'Is it really what you want from me?' she asked huskily.

Hanglin nodded. 'I do – I do.' His penis swelled even more in her hand as she picked the belt up off the floor and stroked it against his tensed buttocks. A little issue dribbled from the tip of his shiny helmet and coated her moving fingers.

'Do you want me to make you come?' Belinda whispered as sexily as she could.

'I'm close already,' he croaked. 'Please beat me now.'

Belinda pumped him a few more times and then squeezed the bulbous plum in her palm. 'Close your eyes,' she whispered, and milked him harder and faster until he erupted impressively and splattered the floor with his seed. He groaned in throes of ecstasy, and she swiftly removed her drawers and stuffed them into his gaping mouth before he could react.

Belinda tiptoed out into the cool night, terrified of bumping into somebody. But nobody was about as she crept down the silent, moonlit street. She stopped only long enough to get rid of the uncomfortable boots. She knew it was best to presume the worst; that the Sheriff would be discovered sooner rather than later. There were only two roads out of town, east and west into open country. She could not run far enough in that time to avoid being run down by him or his deputies, who would obviously split up to search both roads simultaneously. But Belinda was a clever girl from a resourceful family. Instead of heading out of town she went only a few buildings down the street and crawled under the wooden sidewalk. From there she wriggled in until she was beneath the raised building itself. They would never imagine her to be so near, and she would wait until the following night before sneaking off westwards.

No sooner had she settled down than she heard

footsteps coming along the sidewalk. Her eyes widened as she heard the voices. It was the Sheriff and Elizabeth Ladyfield!

'Are you sure she's gone?' asked the conniving woman.

'Yep,' replied Hanglin confidently. 'Worked a treat. She thinks she's escaped. Won't be back for fear of being hanged or locked up for life. Your reputations are safe.'

'It was clever of you to acquire her for us like that,' said the redhead sweetly. 'We each found her utterly irresistible from the moment she arrived here, and she was certainly worth the wait. How did you discover her intended had been murdered?'

'From one of the girls – Jennifer. Got her to befriend Belinda and dig up whatever she could. I was able to make up that murder warrant shit and she believed it. Yep, Jennifer did me well.'

Belinda felt empty. Even her only friend had betrayed her. She stared bleakly into the gloom.

'Are you sure she believed the story about a dungeon under your office?' Elizabeth said. 'We could not afford for her to return telling tales of how we enjoyed ourselves at her expense. The gossip just would not do.'

'Don't worry, Miss Ladyfield,' the Sheriff assured her. 'She'll probably die out there without food and water. Forget her.'

'Very well, if you say so.'

'I do. Anyway, how's about that reward you promised if my clever plan worked?'

'Of course, Sheriff,' the woman said. 'It will be my pleasure to administer the punishment our dear Miss Hopeworth failed to deliver.'

'Elizabeth,' said the Sheriff, 'you are an angel.'

'Just be sure of one thing,' she warned as they walked away and their voices faded. 'Make sure that young lady isn't still around. If you see her, get her out of town and kill her…'

Betrayed, tricked, and beaten, Belinda now also realised she had lost all her savings; she could not be seen in Golden Seat ever again and they were in the bank. The past six weeks had all been for nothing.

She crept out of town feeling extremely sad and alone. If she stayed she would die – if she left she would probably die. Not much of a choice. She sobbed and stumbled westwards until fatigue drew her to the stony ground and she plunged into restless unconsciousness.

Chapter Nine

Belinda knew the sun was high even before she opened her eyes, but thought herself delirious when she heard and recognised a guttural voice.

'The lord taketh away and the lord giveth back.'

Thonnig! Her eyes blinked open. The Danish wagon train was stopped close by and Thonnig was staring down at her.

'We were glad to find the road again,' he said. 'We did not think to find you too.'

In a pair of grudgingly loaned shoes to protect her feet and wearing only her blouse and short leather skirt, Belinda stumbled along all afternoon shackled behind Thonnig's wagon.

Anna sat in the back watching Belinda with contempt. She made frequent shows of drinking mugs of water with great satisfaction, knowing how parched Belinda must be in the heat and the dust.

They did not stop until dusk, and it was fully dark by the time they had formed a square and lit a fire. Belinda was ignored and left manacled to the wagon. Exhausted, she took the opportunity to lie down, and was just dozing when she heard movement.

Anna and Thonnig were moving stealthily around the wagon towards her, looking back to make sure they hadn't been seen by their comrades. They knelt down beside her, and each put a finger to their lips to warn her to be quiet.

'We have come to help you,' Thonnig whispered. 'The others are angry because you ran off with savage atheists and left us to work on the Sabbath.' Belinda started to protest but Anna clamped a hand over her mouth as Thonnig continued. 'They are so enraged by your putting our eternal souls at risk that they are talking of striping you with a red-hot iron.'

Belinda gasped at the fearsome thought. Anna removed her hand.

'We can help you,' whispered Thonnig conspiratorially. 'I am still the leader and they will listen to me.'

'Please, talk to them,' urged Belinda.

'We will help you if you will help us,' said Anna.

'What do you mean?' Belinda had a fair idea what she meant, and her suspicions were quickly confirmed.

'If you agree to permit us to take our pleasure without fear of betrayal,' said Thonnig, 'I will persuade them to exact a more reasonable punishment.'

Belinda wasn't sure if he was telling the truth about the branding, but it would do no harm to be safe. She'd been through too much to be troubled by anything this weird couple had in mind. She despised these hypocrites, but self-preservation was very much the order of the day. 'Very well,' she acquiesced quietly.

Thonnig and Anna exchanged sly smiles. He shuffled in the dirt until his knees nudged against Belinda's shoulder. Opening his trousers with clumsy haste he fished his awakening penis into the open where it bobbed above her face. He masturbated until he was fully erect, and then crouched over her on all fours and slowly pumped his hips and slid his penis across her soft lips. At the same moment Anna's fingers stroked their way beneath the short leather skirt and found her swollen and moist labia. They cleverly found her clitoris and coaxed it beautifully. Belinda's thighs lolled apart and she sighed deeply. As her lips peeled apart Thonnig astutely altered the angle of his hips and sank into her unguarded mouth until his pubic hair cushioned against her hot face. Belinda sucked as hard as she could to prevent herself from choking. She felt Anna straddle her leg and grind her own soaking vagina against her knee. She could hear the couple struggling to suppress their groans of pleasure when there was a sudden and awful interruption.

'Father!' It was Jens. 'Mother!'

The weight and warmth of both bodies instantly left Belinda and her mouth gaped. The three of them looked up in shock and saw the equally horrified faces of Jens and the girl Helle staring down at them from the back of the wagon...

'And her evil powers have worked their demonic ways upon us and brought shame to two loving parents in the eyes of their son and a sweet god-fearing girl.'

Thonnig was concluding his condemnation to the other seven adults in the group. They were sitting on boxes in a half-circle around Belinda and the hypocritical speaker. Jens and Helle stood glumly at the back, and Belinda noticed the pretty blonde's tear-streaked face.

Upon being discovered Thonnig had shown a great gift for quick thinking. He had roared 'Satan!' and immediately shouted for the other couples to run to see how the evil Belinda had corrupted them. As a consequence Jens and Helle were to be beaten in front of the congregation, 'To expunge from their minds the terrible wickedness they had witnessed when Thonnig and Anna had fallen victim to the evil witch.'

Thonnig ordered them both to come forward and strip naked in front of everyone, and they then had to stand in awkward and obedient silence while the self-appointed jury studied them with contempt.

Belinda's anger rose at the thought that they hadn't even done any wrong, and her pity increased as she gazed upon their unblemished pale bodies.

Thonnig decided he would attend to Helle and that the girl's mother should therefore be the one to punish his son. Helle's mother was a powerful looking blonde. She came forward, sat on a box and beckoned Jens. Thonnig took a similar position facing her and ordered Helle to him. The naked teenagers stood with heads bowed, the girl with the man and the boy with the woman.

Thonnig gripped Helle's thighs with his thumbs close to but not quite touching her sweet blonde patch of curls. 'You have been corrupted by vile wickedness, and it must be driven from you,' he pronounced with great piety. Then with an expression of gravity which Belinda knew to be a despicable sham he drew the teenager across his lap and tight against the bulge that Belinda could see in the flickering glow from the campfire.

The big blonde said the same to Jens and gripped his thighs, and Belinda's cheeks blushed with embarrassment for the youth as his lovely penis lurched and bobbed at the touch. She could remember the feel and taste of it in her mouth, and felt a little disappointed as he allowed himself to be prostrated over the skirted lap and thus obscured it from view.

Thonnig and the blonde started spanking in unison. He would raise his hand, she would do the same, and they would then strike simultaneously.

Helle wriggled and sobbed under Thonnig's leathery blows until her buttocks glowed pink in the night air. In contrast Jens remained totally impassive and uttered not a sound for the duration of his

136

punishment. Belinda admired his resolve, and could detect great determination in his character. In her eyes he was already more of a man than his father would ever be.

Nobody spoke as Helle and Jens stood up and followed Thonnig and the blonde away from the group and into the surrounding darkness. Belinda silently backed away, dipped beneath a wagon, and peered out into the night. A cloud drifted high above and the barren land was suddenly bathed in silvery moonlight. It was as she guessed. The big woman was kneeling in front of Jens swallowing his penis avidly, while her daughter was kneeling beside her and attending to Thonnig in a similar fashion, though clearly with a great deal less enthusiasm.

Belinda was dismayed for the teenagers, but could not tear her eyes from the immensely erotic scene. Jens understandably came first as the woman lustfully increased her attentions, her head gliding up and down his length from base to tip. He looked at Helle sucking his father, and then gripped her mother's head, stiffened, and groaned loudly. Belinda knew exactly what the woman was tasting, and instinctively licked her own lips enviously. The woman continued sucking and chewing without any loss of rhythm until the drained young cock plopped softly and wetly from her mouth.

Thonnig's imminent orgasm was clearly building, and Belinda was intrigued to watch Helle attending to him with elegant and unexpected expertise. Her fist was wrapped around the base of his cock and she pumped it while her lips and tongue dealt with the top half and the shiny helmet. Belinda knew from her own experience that this clever method would keep the full length of him out of Helle's mouth.

Helle's breasts swayed sweetly against Thonnig's hairy thighs as she toiled diligently, and then he cursed under his breath and stabbed his groin at her innocent face. At that moment the moon slid behind a cloud and Belinda strained to see through the inky darkness. She felt suspended on a wave of excitement. She held her breath and waited, and then the silvery light slithered across the terrain once more and she saw Helle kneeling back on her haunches with Thonnig's brute of a penis dripping seed onto her gently swelling breasts and erect nipples. He was leaning back against a wagon with his face turned up to the dark sky and his chest heaving violently. Jens was staring at him with undiluted venom in his eyes.

Creeping back to the campfire Belinda decided she hated the perfidious Thonnig and Anna more than anyone else she had ever met. The latter, the two remaining couples and Helle's father were waiting when the quartet returned. Thonnig curtly told the teenagers to get dressed and Helle's mother joined her husband.

'It would be a waste to deal with this demon tonight,' Thonnig said to the group, indicating Belinda. 'You have all seen enough punishment to enable you to perform the divine task of procreation with dedication. Go now to your wagons.'

The group mumbled their agreement and hastily dispersed.

Anna embraced Thonnig and, ensuring Belinda was watching, lewdly squeezed his dormant penis through his trousers. 'We had better keep her with us, dear one,' she hissed breathlessly. 'Perhaps it will encourage fresh life into this for me…'

Belinda traipsed along with the little wagon train all day, weary from the endless demands of the contemptible couple through the previous night. She was not manacled, but the hostile countryside rising steadily towards the Rocky Mountains convinced her that she was better off with the religious sect.

She had to do all the work during the midday break whilst the others lay in the cool shade of their wagons. Her only source of comfort was that she was at least heading in the right direction, towards the town of Los Angeles and a new life.

That evening was considerably colder than the one before, due to their steady climb during the day. Belinda wished they would at least have the decency to lend her a long skirt as she huddled as close to the fire as possible. Dinner was over and she was made to stand and listen as, seated piously on their boxes, the sect discussed her forthcoming punishment for being an evil temptress. Helle and Jens sat at the back. They were allowed to listen, but at their ages they had not yet been initiated into the sect and were therefore precluded from contributing to the discussion.

The suggestions were wide-ranging and perverse, and Belinda was dreading one in particular when it was put forward by one of the wives. 'What about the hot iron? Before we were talking about the hot iron, and now it is not mentioned!'

Belinda's heart sank and the familiar sickness rose in her stomach. The gathering muttered and nodded. The woman continued, 'She is the devil in the guise of a whore. She destroys the minds of decent folk and flaunts it in those shameful clothes. Look at that shameful skirt!'

The mood was turning angry; the muttering increased in volume and the nodding increased in vigour. Belinda silently begged Thonnig with her eyes, but that wicked liar merely shrugged indifferently.

Suddenly the whole group fell silent and turned in amazement to Helle as the teenager stood and spoke calmly. 'Brand her.'

'What?' roared Thonnig.

'Brand her. Brand her before she destroys us all. Before she possesses our minds with her evil powers.'

'Helle!' shouted her mother while the rest of the group sat gawking in disbelief. 'What on earth do you think you are doing?!'

Belinda was dumbstruck. How could the lovely girl be so vicious? Was she secretly harbouring vengeful thoughts because Belinda had pleasured Jens with her mouth?

'Brand every part of her with a red-hot iron,' she continued. 'Every part that she could use to lure a man. Brand her so she can never again dare to wear such an obscene skirt.'

Her mother rose and looked at her with fury. 'How dare you address the meeting?!' she raged.

'An uninitiated has spoken,' intoned Thonnig. 'The Law is broken. That is the word of the founder.'

For some minutes after Helle's departure there hung an uneasy silence over the group. Clearly they had never before witnessed such a flagrant display of disrespect from one who should have known better.

Gradually the tension eased a little, and then Thonnig spoke again.

'Our founder also taught us that no true believer may follow the word of an uninitiated.' There were some angry curses in anticipation of what was to follow. 'There can be no branding.'

Belinda sighed with relief, and a tiny smile of encouragement from Jens caught her eye… it also caught Thonnig's.

'There would appear to be some unhealthy collaboration developing between the whore and the younger members of our group,' he said menacingly. 'I propose we teach them a lesson they shall not forget,' he signalled for Belinda to stand before him, 'commencing with her and my son.'

The group agreed with vocal enthusiasm.

'Remove that provocative and blasphemous skirt,' he snarled at Belinda. She obeyed instantly; the man was dangerously unpredictable. 'Now, make a back... Anna, fetch the whip.'

Belinda didn't understand, but the women made her get down on all fours. Jens, knowing exactly what to expect, solemnly removed his trousers, nudged her feet apart, and knelt between her shapely thighs. The group manhandled him until Belinda felt, whether by design or accident she couldn't be sure, his limp penis squeeze into the valley between her buttocks. They then made him lean forward to cover her.

'Protect his back,' she heard Thonnig instruct somebody. 'We cannot risk some stray lashes draining the valuable strength he will need for the remainder of the journey.'

A thick blanket was thrown over Belinda and Jens so that only their heads, thighs, his buttocks, and her flanks were exposed.

'Commence,' she heard Thonnig shout pompously.

There was a wicked swish and Jens grunted and jerked against her. She felt his penis stir as one of the group lay into him with great gusto. A couple of times the leather thongs whipped around his thighs or buttocks and caught Belinda excruciating blows on her inner thighs or lower belly. She squealed in dismay at the fiery pain. She immediately lost count of how

141

many strikes they suffered, but there was a pause while the whip was passed to the next sadistic member of the group, and then the torture started again. Belinda was so dismayed by the brutal and unjust treatment that Jens jerked fully erect between her thighs before she realised what effect the beating was having on them both. Suddenly in a state of arousal far exceeding anything she had known before, Belinda rested her weight on one forearm and, under cover of the blanket, fumbled frantically for his straining cock. Each loud swish and crack of the whip made him stab forward into Belinda's fist, and she gradually worked the swollen tip to the entrance of her vagina. The group shouted their frenzied delight at the entertainment, but it was Jens sinking smoothly inside Belinda rather than the leather thongs curling viciously around her hips and catching the back of her hand that made her yelp and writhe so exquisitely. She managed to catch his swinging balls and massaged them as he rode her beautifully. He laid his full weight on her back, slipped his hands inside her blouse and squeezed her breasts. Her nipples rubbed into his palms and she groaned ever louder. The group increased their encouragement to Thonnig who was applying the last few lashes. None of them suspected what was happening beneath the blanket, and that only served to heighten her excitement. From the pulsing flesh inside her vagina she knew Jens was experiencing the same wonderful sensations. Jens nestled his face into Belinda's hair and she whimpered into the blanket as he flooded her insides and she shuddered beneath him. Her legs trembled uncontrollably and they slumped to the ground. Above them there was much congratulatory kissing and patting of backs.

'Now let that be a lesson to the two of you,' said

Thonnig, slightly out of breath. Belinda lay shielding her eyes and wallowing in the blissful aftermath of her orgasm.

Helle's mother spoke. 'I think we are now eager to go about the work of procreating to fill the world with righteous babies.'

There was unanimous concurrence and the couples drifted away, as always seemed to be the way. Anna snatched Belinda's wrist in a vicelike grip, hauled the unsuspecting girl to her feet, dragged her to their wagon and cuffed her to one of the wheels.

'My dear husband and I will not be needing you tonight,' she hissed contemptuously and unnecessarily in Belinda's ear. 'You worthless piece of trash.'

Although exhausted, Belinda was still awake long after the muffled grunts and groans from the wagons had ceased and been replaced by infuriating snores. She was at last dozing when a movement startled her and a firm yet gentle hand clamped over her mouth. It was Helle, and she had the key to the manacles. She released her and, emphasising silence by putting her finger to her own lips and then to Belinda's, she helped her stand and led her beyond the light of the dying embers. She handed Belinda her leather skirt and signalled that she should put it on. Belinda was stunned by such a turn of events.

'Make haste,' Helle whispered, and led Belinda away from the sleeping camp. One of the spare horses was tethered to a small tree with a blanket over its broad back and a sack of oats slung on either side. 'Walk it quietly for twenty minutes,' Helle whispered. 'Then get on and ride away from here as quickly as you can. With a couple of hours start the wagons will never catch you.'

'But why?' asked Belinda. 'Why are you doing

this? You wanted me branded.'

'Belinda, are you as stupid as they are evil?' smiled Helle, putting her arms around Belinda's waist. 'I did that because I knew their idiotic laws wouldn't permit them to accept my input.'

'Oh, dear Helle, I'm so sorry.' Belinda embraced her. 'You mean you are prepared to accept one of their foul punishments just to save me?'

'I am used to it,' she replied with a shrug. 'Besides, they'll be less harsh with me.' She slipped her hands under Belinda's blouse and stroked her sides. It was nice and gentle, and Belinda reciprocated. 'They've been beating me and Jens ever since I can remember,' Helle explained. 'We're quite used to it all by now.'

The pretty girl felt wonderful, and Belinda's hands inched up and cupped her firm breasts. Belinda was torn between excitement and embarrassment at her own actions when Helle did the same and pinched her erect nipples.

'Jens and I hate them,' Helle said dreamily. 'When we get to California we are going to run away and live together without any pretend religion.'

Her thumbs rubbed Belinda's nipples with unexpected authority. Her hands slipped away and then returned to unbutton Belinda's blouse. Belinda felt the girl's hot breath on her left breast and then her nipple being sucked into the warm wet mouth. A hand wormed beneath her short skirt and a finger expertly found her clitoris.

'Quickly,' she heard Helle urge through swirling emotions. 'We have little time.'

Belinda needed no further encouragement. She sighed softly and clung tightly to Helle as the Danish girl leaned her back against the uninterested horse and brought her to a wonderful orgasm. They clung

144

together for some time, and then Helle pulled away.

'Go now,' she ordered. 'You must not be caught here. God speed, and let us hope Jens and I will meet you again in California.'

Overcome with gratitude and genuine affection, Belinda pulled Helle close and kissed her deeply and with a fervour that shook Belinda herself. She tore herself away with tears in her eyes. 'I'll look out for you,' she said, and led the horse westward into the night.

Chapter Ten

Belinda's life was a succession of ever-increasing misery. This was her predominant thought during the next week as she followed the trails of the pioneers and prospectors through the Rocky Mountains. The way was arduous but clearly defined by the passage of many previous wagons. In the higher altitudes their wheel marks could still be seen frozen in the mud. The days presented breathtaking views, but the vastness and utter loneliness of this mountain wilderness made Belinda feel incredibly insecure and humble.

Every day she offered thanks to Helle for her thoughtfulness in providing the sacks of oats. Not for the horse, there was enough vegetation for him, but for Belinda. Crystal clear ponds and streams were plentiful, allowing her to wash and drink regularly, but only the coarse cereal saved her from starvation. It was dry and full of husks and stalks, but she made the crudest porridge by wetting handfuls of it in mountain streams and crushing it in her palms. It made her retch but it kept her going, especially through the bone-freezing nights when the horse blanket brought little comfort to her scantily clad body.

On the morning of the seventh day, feeling faint from her miserable diet and lack of sleep, Belinda was heartened to see a fork in the road ahead. As a feature it was interesting enough, after a week without any choice of route, but what set Belinda's heart racing dangerously was that the smaller left hand branch went at forty-five degrees from the main trail. Southwest! Belinda had been getting worried about her constant westerly direction, but was this a chance to head the way she wanted – or would it be a long and dangerous dead end?

Impatient at the horse's laboured pace she swung down and hurried to the junction. It was an established track, although not as well trodden as the main route. The sun showed that it did indeed head southwest, with the added attraction of being downhill. Belinda did not take long in making her choice. She quickly turned to fetch the horse, and her heart froze. She was just in time to see him galloping around a bend a few hundred yards back – and with it went the oats. Belinda was terrified at the thought of starvation, and she cursed her stupidity for not tethering the animal in her joy at seeing the new road.

She staggered and stumbled down the southwest path for hours, knowing that death could not be far away. Exhausted, her eyes kept blurring and her mind wandered. She even saw a man sitting on a veranda on a squeaking rocking chair, sipping from a cup and reading a book in the shade of his house. She was hallucinating; dreaming of the suburban English life she would never see again.

'I say, you look as if you could do with a cup of tea!' the man called, cheerily waving his cup at her. A look of concern replaced his smile as he saw Belinda totter, and he hurried onto the trail to take her arm and lead her in. The firmness of his grip brought Belinda's faculties back. He was real! Though the house turned out to be a natural stone porch that led into a large and well-furnished cave. It was unbelievable! Bricks, carpentry and plaster had been used extensively to make the place acceptably comfortable. The wild-haired man set Belinda in an armchair and crouched beside her. 'I am Doctor Gerhardt, the country's only specialist in disorders of the psyche.' He smiled

147

sympathetically at Belinda's bewilderment. 'If you were looking for my clinic, you have found it. And if you were looking for it on foot, in those clothes and without provisions, then you definitely need my help.'

Belinda simply stared at him, mesmerised by his enormous blue eyes and bushy white eyebrows, as he babbled on happily. 'In spite of my excellent English, I am in fact Austrian,' he said. 'But please, I am forgetting my manners – allow me to introduce my assistant, Nurse Lucy Chan.'

As he spoke a lovely oriental woman appeared from an alcove. She smiled at Belinda, who was having serious problems in accepting this turn of events. She was beginning to have sincere doubts about her own sanity.

'I hope you like the uniform,' said the doctor with infectious enthusiasm as Belinda stared. 'One day all nurses will be dressed thus – believe me...' His wistful eyes devoured the vision as they had doubtless devoured it countless times before.

It was the uniform as much as Nurse Lucy's mystical beauty that astonished Belinda. There was no way the design would ever be allowed in any respectable hospitals. Belinda did think the tiny white hat was cute, but the correctness of the short pale blue dress that clung provocatively to the nurse's curvaceous form was highly questionable. There were white buttons down the front from her shadowy cleavage to her smooth thighs. Small lapels started just above her breasts, and to Belinda it was more like a tight coat than a dress.

The strange couple fed Belinda and treated her with consideration while the doctor outlined his eccentric theories. As she relaxed, she learnt that he came from a very old and extremely wealthy Viennese family. It seemed his ancestors found his progressive ideas an embarrassment and financed his Rocky Mountain Psyche Clinic to get rid of him; apparently the remote location helped 'focus the mind'. He was still looking forward to his first paying client, but in the meantime he and Nurse Lucy had welcomed many passing research patients.

'And I am pleased to say they all benefited from my deep insight into the malfunctions of their psyches,' he smiled as he paced up and down. 'Do you know,' he suddenly frowned, 'before coming here most of them did not even know they had a problem!' He smiled again. 'But what about you? What is your problem, my dear... is it sexual?'

Belinda jumped and blushed furiously. Although listening to him, her eyes had been drawn magnetically to the white buttons that struggled to keep the stretched dress fastened over Nurse Lucy's ample bosom, and she realised she had been wondering if the doctor was ever tempted to pop them open and allow the contents to spring free. His words therefore struck deep.

'I told you I have insight, Belinda...' His voice dropped to a hypnotic whisper. 'Come now,' he prompted gently. 'Tell us all about your secret problems.'

'My only problem is that in trying to get to Los Angeles every man and woman I meet seems intent on taking advantage of me,' she said, her relaxed state giving her the confidence to show a little anger.

'A sexual problem,' nodded Doctor Gerhardt. 'Just as I thought.'

'It's not me with the problem, doctor. It's those vile people who need your services, not me.' Privately she considered his unheard of ideas on disorders of the mind to be absolute claptrap. But there was a certain

149

power about him, a force that was drawing her out of herself.

He stopped pacing and slumped into an armchair opposite her. Nurse Lucy knelt next to Belinda's knees and stroked her calves gently. Her touch was such that Belinda could not take offence or stop her. 'Tell the doctor everything,' she said kindly.

It took a considerable time for Belinda to unburden her soul. With the encouragement of both the doctor and the nurse she detailed her encounters from Liverpool to the Rocky Mountains at great length. She felt no embarrassment as she graphically described each sexual incident, nor did she wonder why she spoke so freely as she gazed into the doctor's perceptive eyes.

At last she had told all. There was a silence and a stillness; nobody spoke or moved for some time. Eventually the doctor uncrossed his legs and the spell was broken. Belinda blinked. She noticed there was a pronounced swelling in his trousers where before there had been none, and that the nurse's hand was wedged firmly between her thighs. She didn't mind on either count; he would have been abnormal if he hadn't found her tale highly arousing, and the nurse's touch was more reassuring than sexual.

'You are too fond of sex and you are too fond of pain,' diagnosed the doctor after some further deliberation.

'That's not fair,' retorted Belinda indignantly, although she suspected it might be. So disorientated did his statement make her feel that she didn't really notice the nurse slip her hand from between her thighs and drift away.

'You complain you have been abused.' He clearly sensed another conquest.

150

'Yes.'

'Yet at the slave plantation you raised no objection to what took place?'

Belinda lowered her gaze and remained silent. The doctor shook his head. 'You played very happily with the Boston party,' he pursued relentlessly.

'They plied me with alcoholic drinks,' she protested.

He raised his bushy eyebrows. 'Did you really object to the Danish group's actions at any point? Did you refuse to join in, or threaten to report them at the next town?'

Belinda nibbled her lower lip as he increased the pressure.

'Did you, an intelligent and educated young lady, at any time ask if there was alternative and decent employment available in Golden Seat?'

His words stabbed at Belinda's heart and she now felt worse than at any time since arriving on these inhospitable shores. Her deep shame was crushing her more than the awesome Rockies ever could. This doctor was no quack. He had penetrated her very soul.

'You even admitted, in a light aside, that you might have enjoyed the Indians' attentions were it not for the fear of death.'

Belinda wished the savages had killed her. 'Can you do anything for me?' she whispered, her lips trembling as she fought back the tears.

With impeccable timing Nurse Lucy appeared holding a pen, inkpot and a piece of paper. 'Sign the consent form, my dear,' urged Doctor Gerhardt. 'Place your trust in me. I can save you from yourself with my Repulsion Therapy. It works. Have you ever heard the saying "too much of a good thing"?' Belinda nodded. 'That is exactly how I will cure you. I will turn your

151

own destructive desires against themselves. But you must trust me totally. You must obey me and you must be completely truthful. Do you understand?'

Belinda thought she understood. She took a deep breath and signed the form.

'Excellent,' enthused the doctor, rising.

Belinda looked up and the first thing she saw was his trousers bulging like a ballet-dancer's tights. She blushed and quickly averted her eyes.

'No,' he urged, 'take a good look. You must follow your instincts fully and freely for this to work.'

Belinda didn't know what to think any more, but she slowly lifted her face and gazed upon his distorted white trousers. He was close, and what to do next she had no idea.

'You must feel it,' he whispered, as though reading her befuddled mind. 'You must confront your inner-self.' He reached down, took her wrist, and pressed her palm over the solid lump. It uncoiled and inched up towards his waistline like a snake under cover. Its heat permeated the white material.

'You like it?' he asked, pressing his groin closer.

Belinda pulled her hand away and shook her head.

'You must be truthful,' he said. 'If you are not it will be a waste of time... Do you like it?'

Belinda coloured prettily. 'Yes,' she admitted. Without any prompting she put her hand back and savoured the size and muscularity of the disingenuous serpent.

'We are going to give you an excess of what your infra-psyche craves, so that those secret workings of your mind will be permanently sated.' He spoke with soft reassurance and covered her hand with his own. 'You will never again unwittingly send out signals of your hidden desires. Those concealed lusts will be extinguished like a falling star.'

Entranced by his words Belinda traced the length of the pulsing ridge.

'Take it out,' he murmured. Without hesitation Belinda undid the buttons, a task made harder by the immense pressure straining behind them. 'You must throw yourself into our treatment with full enthusiasm.' His voice trembled slightly with emotion. 'You are under doctor's orders to absorb as much pleasure as possible from our therapies. You already know that intimate sexual contact outside marriage is only moral if it is part of a medical examination, do you not?'

This last comment, by design or otherwise, cleverly unlocked an overwhelming memory in Belinda as she reached into the gaping trousers and tugged his erect penis into view. It was a memory she did not realise was still there. She had forgotten the suppressed excitement in her last year at boarding school when the top form had to have six-weekly examinations by the school's female doctor. A shorthaired middle-aged woman who affected mannish clothing, her long and detailed examinations were supervised by the smiling matron, who by chance lived with the doctor near the school.

Those final year girls who were intimate enough to discuss the examination all agreed that there was only one problem – trying to conceal the orgasm that the wooden-faced doctor's fingers brought them to as she did her final check on their labia. They also agreed there was nothing to be ashamed of as long as a doctor was doing it.

Inflamed by these liberating thoughts Belinda gazed upon his bobbing column without any feelings of guilt and smoothed it back and forth. She shivered with passion as a drop of clear liquid seeped from the tiny hole at the tip. Moaning softly she squeezed the purple head.

'Kiss it, Belinda…' his hushed words were barely audible. 'Worship it.'

The chair creaked slightly as she leaned forward. Her tongue inched out and scooped up the liquid. She could taste his saltiness. Her conscience needed him to demand she proceed, but he remained silent and watched the internal struggle etched on her adorable face; he was not going to make it easy. After a long pause her lips formed a succulent 'O' and pressed against his bursting helmet. The warm kiss increased in pressure, her lips slowly parted, and slipped over the tip and sealed tightly behind his ridge. Her agile tongue dipped into his single eye and tasted more of his seepage.

'Do you like it, my dear?' His voice gave clear evidence of his own arousal. Belinda nodded, the movement making him inhale deeply, but then he suddenly stepped back and left her groping for thin air. She sighed her disappointment. 'Do not worry, my dear,' he soothed. 'You have many more pleasures ahead of you.'

As if reading her thoughts before she had even formulated them herself, the doctor continued quietly, 'You may unbutton Nurse Lucy if you would like to.'

Belinda gasped. Was this enigmatic man a mind reader? She paused to gather her wits. This was all happening so quickly. Feeling somewhat calmer she released the doctor with a wistful sigh and rose to approach the waiting nurse. Without faltering she reached for the taunting buttons and began to undo them. She started with the top one, and her knuckles pressed into the soft yet firm flesh hiding within the tunic. Nurse Lucy stood without emotion as the first three buttons popped open and Belinda slipped her hands inside the uniform and cupped her naked breasts. Belinda, concentrating hard, licked her lips as she felt the twin mounds thrusting up from the nurse's ribcage. Lucy's expression remained impassive, but her hardened nipples betrayed her degree of arousal. With a cocktail of regret and excitement Belinda relinquished her hold and moved to the next button. She was rewarded with a breathless sigh from the oriental beauty as her fingertips fluttered across the erect buds. The button popped with little resistance, as did the next and the next until the tunic hung slightly open to reveal a tantalising glimpse of the dark triangle at the apex of Lucy's thighs. Belinda paused and stared at the beautiful vision. She then pulled the tunic wide, and was admiring Lucy with undiluted wanting when her own short skirt was lifted at the back. She felt the heat of the doctor's penis press between her buttocks as he took her right hand and slipped it between Lucy's golden thighs. She rubbed her finger up and down the lubricated crease as Doctor Gerhardt unfastened her skirt. He stepped back and let it rustle to the ground, then reached around, unbuttoned her blouse and removed that too. Replacing his penis in the cool valley of her bottom he fondled her breasts from behind as she flicked her fingers across Lucy's clitoris with increasing intensity. Suddenly, and just when Belinda thought the three of them were reaching for mutual orgasm's, he pulled her from Lucy. She moved away, and then returned with a low stool. She placed it on the floor and stood on it.

'Watch this,' instructed the doctor, and with his towering erection bouncing before him he approached Lucy. The stool compensated for their differences in height, so that when he stood in front of her his engorged helmet nudged lightly at the centre of her exposed sex.

She parted her unbuttoned tunic and put her hands on her hips to keep it open, and then squatted a little to part her thighs a fraction more. Belinda watched as the doctor pushed the tip of his organ forward. Lucy's vulva resisted, and then opened like a blooming orchid to encircle the very tip of his penis. Almost sick with excitement and envy, Belinda saw the head slowly disappear into the nurse, and then stop. The doctor stayed like that for a few seconds, his shaft fully visible but the head just inside his assistant. Her eyes were shut and she was wriggling herself against it as she kept her balance on the tiny stool.

'Nice or not?' the doctor smiled at Belinda.

'Oh, that's nice doctor…' Belinda whispered softly. 'That's so nice…'

He pulled out of Lucy and indicated that Belinda should change places with her. The nurse stepped down at once and Belinda did as she was told.

She stood naked on the stool and stared hungrily at him. All her inhibitions were suspended. She was convinced that his revolutionary treatment would work. She couldn't see how exactly, but the power that flowed from this man was such as to make her believe that the only way to free herself of her attraction to perverted admirers was to follow his treatment without reservation. These thoughts were not formulated into words in her mind, but took the form of a flash of emotion as the doctor pressed his tip insistently to her cunt.

He wasn't smiling now, she noticed with thumping heart as his hands gripped her buttocks to steady her on the stool. She felt the cheeks of her vulva depress, just as the nurse's had, then peel open and welcome the silky head as it moved in and stopped with its rim on her clitoris. She looked down and, seeing the shining shaft protruding from her, squatted a little as Lucy had done.

'Do you like it?' he asked, moving his hands from her bottom to her nipples.

'Oh yes!'

'Do you like this?' he asked, and Belinda shrieked and jerked as unexpected agony exploded on her bare bottom. She lunged fully onto the rigid penis as the pain shot from her rear to her brain and back in relentless cycles. Holding onto the doctor for support she strained desperately to see what was happening over her shoulder. Nurse Lucy was standing behind her holding a black leather paddle. It contrasted starkly with her delicate hands. Before Belinda could react to protect herself she swung it well back, like a golfer, and swept it in a fast downward curve. Her tunic flew open and the shiny leather cracked once more onto Belinda's backside.

Belinda howled and begged the nurse to stop between sobs.

'Do you like it?' repeated Doctor Gerhardt impatiently whilst grinding against her.

'No,' she whimpered, her breasts heaving against his chest. 'Of course I don't...'

'Oh dear.' He shook his head and tutted like a disappointed father. 'And I thought you were intelligent enough to appreciate the need for absolute honesty...' He gripped her chin and stared into her tear-filled eyes. He gave her a look of deep concern and then kissed her gently on the lips, his penis moving deliciously inside her. Keeping his lips close to hers he murmured quietly, 'Nurse...'

157

With a vicious swish the paddle caught her poor bottom once more. Belinda howled again and teetered on the stool. She would have toppled to the floor, but the good doctor held her tightly around the waist and drove himself even deeper. She could not agree that she liked being beaten, even if the afterglow did somehow heighten the sensuality of the slow piston reaming her insides. Six more times the doctor urged her to admit she loved it. Six more times she sobbed her denial, and six more times the paddle scorched her unprotected buttocks.

'This isn't working,' she pleaded. 'Please – you've got it wrong.'

'Do you know,' said the doctor, studying her closely, 'I think you're telling the truth. We're on the wrong track.'

Belinda gasped and reached for him as he suddenly pulled away, leaving her floundering in a whirlpool of frustration that more than matched the pain in her behind.

'Nurse, a complete change of approach is required,' he said, looking violently annoyed with himself for making such a mistake. He swore loudly and punched one of the chairs with a sudden display of temper that startled and frightened Belinda.

'So sorry,' said Nurse Lucy with a sweet voice that matched her feminine sensuality perfectly. 'We truly thought that was the correct path, but now we see it was leading us in the wrong direction.'

'It did hurt,' pouted Belinda.

'We know. We are sorry. Now we know what to do.' She smiled and stroked Belinda's hips with a silky touch that made her shiver. She closed her eyes, and was not surprised or disappointed when a rigid finger slipped up into her soaking vagina.

'You like it now, yes?' whispered the nurse.

'Yes… I like it now. It's just that…'

'Yes?'

'It's just that you're a woman too.'

Lucy smiled sympathetically. 'Of course I am. Have you never been touched in such a way by another woman?'

Belinda blushed. 'I suppose so, but—'

'Then where's the harm?'

All through this intimate and sensual exchange the doctor observed closely. Belinda considered Lucy's argument for a while. 'I suppose you're right,' she eventually said. 'I'm very tired though, I haven't slept properly for so long. And I need a wash. I can't think very clearly.'

'Of course,' smiled Lucy. 'Forgive us our tardiness. Come.' With a quick glance and smile to the doctor Nurse Lucy led Belinda around an overhang of rock into a more private alcove. There was tub already filled with steaming aromatic water. Obviously her needs had been anticipated. She was left alone to wallow in the luxurious water, and immediately felt ten times better than she had for quite some time. As she stepped from the water Lucy returned right on cue. She held a towel and dried Belinda, her gentle hands patting and stroking more intimately than was perhaps necessary. As Belinda felt herself becoming a little flustered at the sweet touches Lucy stopped and led her to a low double bed. Lucy laid her down on it and covered her with a soft blanket. Belinda felt beautifully warm and relaxed, and with Lucy stroking her brow she quickly drifted into a welcome sleep.

'Do not be alarmed,' Belinda heard as she opened her eyes to find Nurse Lucy naked and kneeling astride her stomach. She wasn't alarmed; nothing much could surprise her any more. And besides, she did find the nurse extremely attractive. She realised she couldn't fully move her arms, and strained to see them bound to the head of the bed by restraints she hadn't noticed before. Her legs seemed to be similarly bound at the ankles. Despite all this she remained calm. She had no idea how long she'd been asleep, but did feel very much refreshed.

The doctor sat in a chair nearby busily scribbling notes.

Lucy crouched lower and kissed Belinda long and deep. 'Do you feel all right?' she asked when she broke away.

'Yes – thank you,' said Belinda.

'Now, we're not going to do anything you won't like,' Lucy went on. 'And remember – everything we do and say is dedicated to your cure and your future happiness.' Belinda nodded and smiled a little uncertainly. Then Lucy took Belinda's left nipple between finger and thumb and squatted lower over the breast. She pulled the nipple to her, stretching the aureole, and did an extraordinary thing; she used the nipple to stimulate her clitoris, flicking it backwards and forwards across the slippery bud. Belinda found it extraordinary not only because it was highly sensual and caused both her nipples to tingle and stiffen, but also because she had never imagined such a technique probable. There was a stillness, broken only by the two females' laboured breathing and the scratch of the doctor's pen on paper. Belinda arched her back slightly to encourage Lucy.

'You are enjoying that,' the doctor stated rather than asked, his eyes unblinking.

Belinda looked at him. 'Yes,' she said clearly. 'It

feels lovely.'

The doctor stood and nodded as though something was formulating in his mind. 'Given the current situation, with whom would you rather be; Nurse Lucy – a woman, or me – a male?'

Belinda moaned as Lucy massaged her other breast. 'That's not a fair question,' she protested.

'Whom?' persisted the doctor, placing his notes on the chair.

He was stirring dormant desires within Belinda that she had always kept suppressed; refusing to accept the possibility that they could ever exist, let alone be accepted. Did she really prefer women to men? She had felt immense affection, bordering on sexual attraction, towards some females it was true. Helle for example. But that was surely a perfectly natural inclination – wasn't it? Oh, she was so confused. 'I couldn't say,' she whispered as she writhed under the lovely nurse.

The doctor approached the bed and pulled his semi-erect penis out of his trousers. 'Try,' he urged.

Belinda gazed at the pulsing flesh and couldn't deny her desire to feel it, either in her mouth or between her legs. 'Both,' she compromised. 'I would like to be with you both equally.'

The doctor smiled with satisfaction. 'Just as I predicted.'

Belinda barely heard him any longer such was the pleasure she was enjoying from the clever Lucy and the sight of that thickening stalk.

'Now,' he continued anyway. 'We're going to perform a technique which has always proved extremely successful in the past. It is to teach you self-denial.' Belinda was beyond caring what they did as more of her breast disappeared inside Lucy. 'Nurse

Lucy… are you ready?'

'Yes doctor,' she said, and to Belinda's immense disappointment she climbed off her and lay by her side. Although so tantalisingly close there was not one inch of their bodies that touched. Belinda yearned to feel her feminine softness again.

The doctor placed a cushion under Belinda's head enabling her to see more, and then checked the silky bonds that held her wrists and ankles apart. When satisfied he undressed, flaunting his surprisingly fit body before the trussed girl, and then stood over her with his penis bobbing above her red face. 'Nurse Lucy and I are going to indulge ourselves now. You will watch. Do you understand?'

Belinda was mortified. She was so acutely excited, and now she had to suffer the indignity and frustration of watching these two enjoying the delights she so desperately wanted – and needed. This was so unfair!

The doctor, still smiling enigmatically, moved around the bed and gently pulled Lucy's ankles apart. The oriental beauty lay passively staring at Belinda as he climbed between her legs and knelt, aiming his penis at her silky black pubes. Without any hesitation he lowered himself and entered his assistant with one effortless thrust. Lucy's eyes closed in unison with the entry, and when he was fully embedded they opened again and stared mistily at the girl by her side, a slight smile dancing across her lips. Belinda's fingers clenched and unclenched and she tensed in the frustrating bonds. She despised the two for teasing her so, but she could not tear her eyes away from the wonderfully erotic display. She wondered how many women had suffered this torment on this very same bed before her. She hated the doctor and his nurse… but she wanted them – both.

162

The doctor made love to Lucy slowly and for a long, long time. Belinda marvelled at his stamina and powers of self-control. She watched mesmerised as his bottom rose and fell majestically without faltering. A glossy sheen gradually coated their bodies. The doctor first kissed Lucy's brow, then her cheeks, her chin, and then on down to her breasts and nipples. All the while her dreamy gaze searched Belinda's eyes and laid bare her very soul.

'We will come now,' the doctor at last broke the magical silence, but Belinda wasn't sure which of them he was addressing. With that he increased the speed of his thrusts. Lucy arched and urged herself up to him. His buttocks hollowed, and he raised himself on straightened arms. Both he and Lucy watched Belinda, and then they shuddered together. No other expression of joy or delight was forthcoming. The lovemaking had been tender and highly erotic to watch, but the final release was clinical – as though they were concluding an experiment.

The doctor and Lucy climbed off the bed and dressed without a word to each other. The whole scene was bizarre, and Belinda felt her uncertainties returning.

'Would you mind, Nurse Lucy?' the doctor said as he picked up his notes. With that the nurse moved beside Belinda, reached between her legs and rubbed her soaking and excited lips. Belinda was shocked to realise just how highly charged she was, and she exploded at the first delectable touch.

'Very good,' the doctor said. 'We are making progress. A few weeks here, my dear, and you'll be just fine.'

'Sleep some more,' whispered Lucy. 'It will soon be morning, and then we can continue with your treatment.' Belinda did not want to sleep; she was beginning to think she was here not for her own good, but for the selfish gratification of these two, but the gentle voice soothed her and she drifted away again...

When she awoke her limbs were free to move. She rose and stretched. Her clothes were laid on a chair, so she dressed and ventured off to explore – or perhaps to get away. How she could do that without a horse she wasn't sure, but perhaps an idea would develop. She heard voices and peeped around the overhang of rock. Curse it! The doctor and Nurse Lucy were in the main area, between her and the exit. Belinda crept as close as she could without being seen. The doctor was speaking.

'She is an absolute dream, Lucy. We'll go through in a short while and proceed with the next stage.'

'I can't wait,' cooed Lucy huskily.

'Is everything ready?'

She grinned. 'It is... more than ready.'

Belinda trembled. She didn't like the possible implications of what they were saying, or the lurid manner in which it was being said.

'How long do you think we can keep her here?' said the doctor.

'We can make it last a few weeks without suspicion,' replied the nurse with surprising authority. 'You just be sure to keep finding new problems, and leave the rest to me. When I've finished the dear girl will not want to leave me.'

'Excellent!' beamed the doctor.

Belinda's legs buckled upon hearing their conspiratorial exchange and she stumbled out into the open.

'What?' The doctor spun to stare at her.

'What are you doing there?!' snapped Lucy with a venom that shocked Belinda. 'How much did you hear?' She approached the gawping girl menacingly.

'I – I didn't hear anything!' blurted Belinda. 'But I – I'm leaving, I'm afraid. I don't think I need your treatment any more. But thank you for everything, you have both been very kind, and I don't know what I would have done...' she knew she was rambling and stopped as Lucy snatched her arms.

'You go when we say,' the oriental hissed. Her change of demeanour was difficult to accept. 'You signed the consent form. That means you stay with us until we decide you can go.'

'Everything all right here, doc?' boomed a voice from the entrance, and a man in a dusty blue uniform strode into the chamber.

'Captain Harding!' stammered the doctor, trying to hide his agitation. He rose and enthusiastically shook the gloved hand of the cavalry officer. 'Yes, of course, everything's fine. It's good to see you again. Come, take a seat – have a drink. Lucy, would you mind?'

Lucy threw Belinda a vicious warning stare and resumed her subservient deportment. She poured two whiskeys.

'What you got there, doctor?' asked the heavily whiskered cavalry officer, looking at Belinda's short cowgirl skirt. 'I never heard there was a circus around these parts,' he sneered sarcastically. A rugged and equally dusty Sergeant followed him in, and roared with laughter at his officer's immense wit and at Belinda's discomfort.

'Sergeant Riley,' the doctor welcomed him with equal vigour as Lucy handed them each a drink. 'You are looking well. I trust you enjoyed your leave?'

'Ah, you should've been with us, doc,' boomed the

Sergeant.

'We stopped three nights at Golden Seat,' said the Captain. Belinda's heart thumped and she guiltily looked at the ground.

'What a place, doctor,' laughed Riley.

'Apparently we missed the best,' Harding continued. 'There'd been a girl there who'd made quite a name for herself. Seems she was a bit of an expert at most anything a man could want.'

'Yeah,' added Riley ruefully, 'but she'd gone by the time we got there.'

The doctor noticed Belinda blushing brightly.

'You should come with us next time, doc,' Riley winked. 'You'd love it.'

'Good heavens, no,' laughed the doctor. 'A respectable man like me...?'

Belinda took a deep breath. 'Which... which way are you going, please?' she asked timidly, spotting a chance to get away from the mad doctor and his nurse.

'Back to Fort Choquaw,' answered Harding. 'Four days' hard riding, but we got all the home comforts and it's mainly downhill now.'

'Which direction would that be?' she asked politely. From the corner of her eye she saw the vile couple bristle.

'Southwest, miss. Between the foot of the Rockies and the southern end of Death Valley.' He gazed at her thoughtfully – and appreciatively. 'You're welcome to come along, if that's what you're getting at...'

Chapter Eleven

There were four ordinary cavalry soldiers slouching outside as Belinda left the mountainside clinic with Harding and Riley. They were loafing by ten horses; one for each soldier and four spares that also carried their equipment and supplies.

The scruffy gang looked a thoroughly unsavoury and dangerous bunch, thought Belinda, but dangerous in a criminal rather than a military way. She decided that any one British Hussar could confidently take on the whole platoon. They looked like the sort of soldiers who might be very good at creeping up on someone and shooting or stabbing them in the back before running away. Or, more likely, just running away.

But they were spirited enough in raising a drooling hullabaloo when they lay their hungry eyes on Belinda, and the trooper who helped her onto one of the spare horses predictably took the opportunity to stuff his hand up the back of her skirt to molest her buttocks. She knew it was pointless to object, and decided it would be best to simply humour them and pander to their egos.

The doctor and his nurse had raised no objection when Belinda left, but then, how could they? They were clearly concerned for their image of respectability. At last she could afford a tiny smile – if only a smile of relief; she was riding southwest on a good horse, and she even had an armed escort of sorts, even if they were so obviously a gang of spineless ne'er-do-wells.

Her opinion of them did not improve during the first twenty-four hours. All day, and once camped, all evening, she was subjected to a barrage of sexual jokes, comments on her clothing, and various invitations to sample the sexual prowess of the troopers. She wished there could be a law against this persistent sort of verbal imposition, but knew that was an impossible dream. She was annoyed that the Captain was just as bad, albeit in a more educated way. She was also disturbed at the informality between the officer and his men, a further sign of an unsoldierly bearing. She feared he would not wield enough authority to protect her should they consider suiting lewd comment to unimaginable deed. On the other hand she did appreciate the blankets, beans, and hot coffee they provided in generous amounts.

At noon the next day her opinions toward them were unequivocally changed.

The breezeless heat had temporarily quietened their banter as they rode along, and Belinda was pondering her stay at the clinic. In spite of her disillusionment at the end, she still thought the doctor had delved skilfully into the deeper recesses of her mind. She felt different somehow; more aware perhaps. She didn't know what it was exactly.

She was wrenched ruthlessly from her thoughts by an arrow thudding into one of her horse's panniers, just by her knee. The sudden and terrible danger was immediately emphasised by a blood-curdling scream from behind. Her horse reared up violently, its eyes rolling, and Belinda clung around its neck for dear life. Despite her panic she realised the scream had come from the skinniest and most loathsome of the troopers as he galloped past her at breakneck speed, apparently without any consideration for his own safety. In no time he reached the wooded defile just ahead and in one graceful movement unsheathed a vicious knife and

168

threw himself from his horse. The sun flashed off the broad blade as an Indian's throat was slashed from ear to ear, and then arched upwards to bury itself in the groin of another hideously painted warrior. Within seconds the rest of the troop had charged heads-down and hollering into the ambush area to clash ferociously with a dozen mounted Indians and more on foot. The motley patrol fought like Satan's own tigers, booting the running foe in the face whilst hurling themselves from their horses to bring down the mounted foe. The furious slaughter seemed to last for hours, but it was only a minute or so before the victorious troopers had killed thirteen of the ambushers and sent the remaining half a dozen galloping off in a panic. Even then three soldiers leapt onto their horses and chased the fleeing band. They shot another two before six rapid signal shots from the Captain's revolver summoned them back for fear of a further ambush.

Belinda regretted everything she had doubted about their military capabilities. These men had no concept of defence – they should have checked the narrow wooded passage – but with their proven instincts of pure attack caution was obviously irrelevant. Her own terror ebbing as the jubilant troopers cleared the track of bodies, it occurred to her that whilst the British Hussars planned carefully before going in to be killed, this lot just went in to be killed.

Suddenly they were heroes. Her heroes, because she would surely have been dead without them. Now everything she had loathed became noble. Scruffy they were, but she could now see their slouching and smirking were the relaxed signs of battle-hardened confidence. That night she insisted on boiling the beans and coffee while they had a deserved rest.

As the small group sat and lay quietly around the

campfire, Belinda could see in their eyes that they were hoping to be rewarded for their valour; hoping she would show her appreciation. She was surprised that, apart from the previous verbal abuse and the hand up her skirt, they were not forcing themselves upon her. Had they done so she would have instinctively fought to repel them, but because they did not her own curiosity and excitement were building rapidly. Increasingly she was hoping they would make advances, and fought to suppress a shiver of anticipation when they at last did so.

'Hey, girl,' Riley broke the silence. 'Are you going to grant us knightly champions of your honour a little thank you, or what?'

All eyes, including the Captain's, were on her. Why should she withhold her favours from brave men who had saved her life when she had already given those same favours to the world's lowest vermin? She studied each man pensively. They were certainly nothing to look at and their bodily odour left much to be desired, but their unexpected daring gave them a sexual quality she found highly electrifying and could not deny. 'Yes...' she whispered above the crackle and spits of the fire, '...of course I will.'

The soldiers deliberately slowed their journey to give them time to extract as much pleasure from it as possible. Captain Harding said he would report to the Colonel that the Indians had held them up for two days.

Eventually they were out of the Rocky Mountains and riding across a great plain. Belinda was concerned to notice an increasing tension amongst her courageous and wonderfully virile companions. They consistently asked the Captain if he was sure he could cover up for their being two days overdue. He assured them he would deal with the Colonel, but there was an uneasy edge to his voice too.

They rode across the plain for most of the day and then, towards the end of the afternoon, Belinda made out the fort shimmering in the distant heat.

'Just remember you're a civilian and you don't have to answer any of the Colonel's questions,' Harding told her. 'Leave all the talking to me.'

Soon they were within half a mile of the crude wooden stronghold set in the middle of nowhere, and Belinda squinted at the welcoming party standing at the open gates. 'Indians!' she screamed and turned in horror to Captain Harding. 'The fort's been overrun by Indians!' She was panic-stricken. Their refuge was in the hands of savages who would surely murder them all. Even the courage and skill of her escort would be no match for large numbers on this open ground.

'Don't worry,' he chuckled. 'They're friendly.'

'Oh,' said Belinda, feeling silly.

It certainly was a dishevelled rabble of natives that parted to allow the party through the large gates. She had never seen such miserable faces. Men and women were almost identical, dressed from neck to toe in smelly suede skins, with greasy plaited hair. The doleful children looked hungry and unwashed.

There was no sign of any other soldiers in the fort as the party rode slowly to a wooden building that stood out from the rest because of its short flight of steps up to the door and the flags that hung limply on either side of the entrance. There was a tense atmosphere as the four troopers formed a straight rank with the Captain and the Sergeant to the front. Belinda, sitting on her horse to one side, wanted to ask what was going on, but dare not. The silence was almost deafening as they waited, and then the door burst open and the Colonel stomped out – a terrifying figure of a man.

Smartly dressed in grey trousers beneath a long blue jacket, he fixed his cold dark eyes on Captain Harding.

'Patrol returning from leave Colonel!' the Captain barked, saluting smartly.

The Colonel returned the salute with equal briskness, but did not reply. He stared hard at the Captain, and then at Belinda. His expressionless eyes flitted over her breasts and legs. They unnerved her greatly.

'You are two days overdue, Captain Harding,' he growled menacingly.

'Yes sir! Delayed by savages, sir!'

'Delayed by savages for two days?'

'Yes sir!' The Captain fixed his eyes over the Colonel's head at the building behind. 'They had us pinned down, but we finally got the better of them – sir!'

'So,' said the Colonel with a noticeable tone of disbelief. 'You allowed yourself to be besieged for two days by a rabble of peasants, Captain?' Captain Harding looked ill at ease. 'And where, precisely, did this siege take place? I can think of no suitable spot along that trail to hole up for two days.'

The Captain had not prepared his story well enough, and the Colonel continued to tear all excuses to shreds.

'You were not besieged, Captain Harding, you were besotted,' said the Colonel with astounding astuteness. 'This...' he waved his gloved hand dismissively towards Belinda and curled his lip contemptuously, 'this female is why you and your troop have been absent without leave. And now she has compelled you to lie to a superior officer. Well, you've had your fun and now you must pay. The six of you will each publicly receive six lashes of the whip.'

Belinda was horrified at such unfair treatment. The exhausted men had protected her without due consideration for their own safety. Now she must reciprocate. 'Colonel.' She cleared her throat and steeled herself. 'If I may speak. These men fought with astonishing bravery – and won. Any subsequent dalliance on their part was entirely my fault and I beg you not to punish them for it.' She felt quite safe in accepting full responsibility, knowing that she was not subject to military law.

The Colonel stared at her with disgust. 'I am fully aware of your role in this matter, madam, and I wish to discuss that with you. If, of course, you have no more interruptions to offer?'

Belinda shook her head. This man had an unnerving air of menace and penetrating perception. She could now see why the troopers were more afraid of him than they were of a gang of savages.

'Kindly dismount and follow me,' he snapped. 'The rest of you will dismiss and attend to your horses. You will muster here in precisely one hour to await your punishment.'

Belinda, flustered and apprehensive, hurried after the Colonel as he strode back into the building.

The interior was a single large room that incorporated his office, sitting room and bedroom. The walls were decorated with military and Indian memorabilia, and a stuffed wolf's head. He told Belinda to close the door behind her and, as she did so, took off his jacket and sat behind his desk. He lit a fat cigar and clamped it between white teeth. He fixed her with his gimlet eyes. Long minutes passed in silence.

'A beautiful Englishwoman of less than twenty years old,' he eventually said quietly. 'Wandering in

173

the Rocky Mountains dressed in an astonishingly indecent and inappropriate manner. Would you care to explain yourself?'

'Well sir,' began Belinda timidly, 'it's an awfully long story, but I – I sort of lost my real clothes and these were all someone could spare me.' She could see her vagueness was not impressing him. 'But the main thing is that I am trying to get to Los Angeles to find my uncle.'

'What is your name, young lady?'

'Belinda Hopeworth, sir,' she answered honestly.

'Belinda Hopeworth – and you are looking for an uncle?' He folded his arms across his broad chest, leaned back in his chair, and blatantly studied her delicious curves more closely. He beckoned her to approach, and had her stand in front of his knees. He took her hands in his. 'Belinda,' he said, 'I think your search is over.'

Her heart leapt. 'You mean… you mean you are my uncle?' she exclaimed with wide-eyed incredulity.

'No,' he snorted, and a hint of humanity almost creased his stern face. 'But I am an uncle. I have an adorable niece about your age. We used to get along real fine until she was seventeen and her mother sent her off to Europe for education.' He gazed upon her breasts. 'I kinda miss her.'

Belinda blushed at her silly outburst. 'I am truly sorry to hear that, sir,' she said sincerely. 'But I don't quite see—'

'Perhaps we could help each other,' he interrupted.

'Help each other? How sir?'

He rolled the fat cigar from one side of his mouth to the other. 'You clearly don't want the men to be punished. Your loyalty is highly touching and commendable.'

174

'Thank you. They did save my life, after all.'

'Quite.' His jaw tightened as he clamped the cigar even tighter. 'Why don't you sit on my knee, and we'll discuss the matter.'

If there was a chance of getting him to change his mind about the whippings she would do what she must to seize it. She turned sideways to sit on his lap.

'No,' he stopped her, and then pulled gently on her hands so that she had to straddle his thighs. 'Now sit,' he instructed. Belinda found the smooth material of his well-tailored trousers to be quite sensual as it brushed her inner thighs and caressed her sex beneath the skirt. He then casually rested his hands on her thighs, and his fingertips and thumbs inched, almost accidentally, under the hem. The touch sent a secret thrill of nervous pleasure up her spine. The arms of the chair inhibited her position slightly, so he squirmed a little lower in the chair until she was lodged over his groin. She could feel his heat radiating through the trousers. Cigar smoke curled around them both, and Belinda found the rich scent quite pleasant.

'Now,' the Colonel croaked. 'Those soldiers are as fine a fighting force as you'll find anywhere in this land. Between you and me, I can't blame them for being led astray by your abundant charms.' His gaze fell on her breasts again and he squeezed her thighs. Belinda didn't know whether to accept his words as a compliment. 'Trouble is, as I'm sure you know, I have no authority to deal with civilians – except in exceptionally serious matters. Since I cannot punish you, I have no choice but to punish them as an example to everyone else under my command.'

'I see,' Belinda whispered.

'On the other hand, if you, as a matter of honour, were to accept full responsibility for their

175

waywardness and voluntarily take their punishment yourself I would feel obliged to cancel their sentence.'

Belinda was torn. In theory she saw the proposal as an ideal solution in terms of honour and fairness, but she didn't relish the thought of being flogged – particularly not in front of the whole fort. On the other hand six lashes was not excessive, and would at least repay those men for their chivalry. So deep in thought was she that she was barely aware of him fumbling beneath her skirt with his trouser fastenings.

'Before you make a final decision on such a grave matter,' he continued, with the cigar seemingly lodged permanently between his yellow teeth. 'It is important you understand that I am an honourable gentleman and officer...'

Belinda had her doubts about that.

'...and am therefore prepared to reduce the number of lashes by one third, if you are prepared to show your gratitude to such a magnanimous gesture.'

Four lashes. She could cope with that, and honour would be satisfied. 'Very well,' she nodded.

'A wise decision.' He placed the cigar in an ashtray on the desk and licked his lips. 'Undo your blouse.' His eyes bulged as they followed her fingers moving methodically down her front, undoing the buttons as they went. Soon the white blouse was tugged from the skirt and held open for him to feast upon the firm beauty of her breasts. He swallowed hard, and then startled Belinda by latching onto a nipple and devouring it as though near starvation. She could smell his greasy hair tonic as he chewed and salivated over her. More fumbling beneath the skirt and she gasped as she felt a stiff column spring against her thighs. She held his head to prevent herself from tumbling backwards onto the floor, and he obviously interpreted

176

this as an indication of her mounting passions. He buried his face between her breasts and inhaled her wholesome scent as he wormed his hands beneath her bottom and jiggled her into the required position. Belinda accepted the inevitability of her predicament, so she closed her eyes and allowed him to do as he wished. He was snorting in her cleavage like a pig, and then she felt something like a plum peel open her sex-lips. Hands pressed down on her hips and she sank onto his vertical rod. Their position allowed the Colonel to penetrate her deeply, and she could not withhold a long, satisfied sigh. Her fingers entwined in his greasy hair and she guided an erect nipple into his hungry mouth. He cupped her bottom again and guided her up and down his gnarled length. She threw her head back and almost instantly shuddered into a wonderful orgasm.

Belinda wanted to sit quietly and wallow in the divine pleasures the Colonel had evoked, but he had different ideas. Without consideration he lifted her and lay her back onto his desk. Her legs were pulled apart and her bottom hauled forward until it was just on the edge of the cool mahogany. The blouse lay open and the skirt was nothing more than a roll of leather around her waist. Dropping his trousers but keeping his shirt on as if she wasn't worth the bother of undressing completely, he stepped close, his penis peeping from between the shirttails, and entered her. Standing tall and staring down imperiously he began to fuck her, the only sound in the room being the quiet creak of the desk. He reached forward and squeezed her breasts, almost painfully, and just enough to let her know who was in charge. Despite Belinda's attempts to control her lust she felt it rising inexorably once again. Why had he not yet come? Was she inadequate? Her brow

177

furrowed as she concentrated hard and squeezed her vaginal muscles around the invading stalk, but as his thrusting hips increased their tempo it was Belinda who arched off the desk and came for a second time.

Without respite and in a confused dream she was rolled over and her feet kicked wide apart. Her trembling legs barely supported her swooning body. The man was insatiable! She was pressed forward until her perspiring breasts sank onto the pink blotting pad, and then a draw slid open. The skirt was again folded up around her waist. Her buttocks were prised apart and a cool cream was coated into the deep valley and around her private entrance. Belinda had never imagined that such a sexual act was ever indulged in, but was too breathlessly excited to complain. She gripped the edge of the desk as the plum pressed against her tiny hole, and then whimpered as the ring of muscle relaxed and the column slowly stretched and filled her. Waves of rapture washed over her as the Colonel's shirttails and pubic hair nestled against her bottom. A hand gripped her shoulder and pulled her up until she leaned uncertainly against him. She gasped as the new position increased the sensations in her bottom. Buttons dug into her back. Fingers found her clitoris and nipples. They teased and stroked in unison, and soon Belinda's head fell back on his shoulder and her hips ground against the statuesque officer.

'I'm going to come again,' she whispered as her breasts wobbled in the first throes of orgasm. 'Please... come with me.'

The Colonel grunted and pulled her harder onto his erection. That was enough for Belinda. She bit her lip and came over and over again. Her beautiful lean body was as taut as longbow. Unaware of what she was doing she reached up and passionately curled her fingers into his hair. His face registered no expression as the young lady in his arms gradually calmed and slumped against his chest breathing deeply.

The Colonel draped her over the desk, pulled up his trousers, and straightened his uniform.

'Come on then,' he growled and kicked her foot. 'Get yourself ready.'

'Ready?' Belinda mumbled, rising from the desk and feeling totally drained. 'Ready for what?'

The Colonel lewdly gripped the erection, which still clearly bulged within his trousers. 'Your punishment, of course. It's time for you to give me some *real* pleasure.'

'I – I don't understand,' stammered Belinda.

'You will… believe me, you will…'

Without allowing her to cover her modesty the Colonel gripped her arm unnecessarily tightly, opened the door, and pushed her to the top of the steps outside. She squinted against the huge orange sun as it sank below the distant range of mountains. It seemed the fort's full complement was mustered on the small parade ground, with the six accused fallen in at the front. Belinda blushed as she tried to cover her breasts with the unbuttoned blouse.

'Men!' the Colonel boomed. 'As you are all well aware, I earlier sentenced each of these six soldiers…' he indicated Harding, Riley, and the others, '…to six lashes of the whip for being two days absent without leave! However, the true culprit, this civilian female, has accepted full responsibility and has agreed to receive a reduced sentence on their behalf! They are therefore excused on this occasion! But mark my words – they, or any of the rest of you, will not be so lucky if there is a next time!'

The reprieved looked up at Belinda in astonishment.

Upon the Captain's order the Sergeant dismissed them, whereupon they joined their gathered colleagues and received many a slap on the back.

Without further ado the Colonel marched Belinda to a post in the centre of the small parade area, muttered to a tall Indian, and then handed her over to him. He then beckoned to a lovely squaw, led her back up the wooden steps to his office, and slammed the door.

Belinda was astonished by his behaviour, but had little time to think as the Indian made her remove her grimy blouse and skirt. He then tied her hands high above her head to the post, and as she gazed fearfully over the heads of the gawping troops she could just make out the silhouette of the Colonel standing behind the girl and watching from a window. The lamps in his office remained unlit.

Belinda's attention was drawn back to the Indian, who was now pressing unnecessarily close behind her and holding a fearful looking whip. He sadistically drew the leather handle across her cheek. 'Twenty-four, the Colonel tell me,' he hissed.

Belinda shuddered. 'No – I think you've got that wrong. I'm only supposed to have four lashes.'

'Twenty-four.' The Indian was not to be argued with.

'But…' and then the truth hit her like a stampeding herd of longhorns. She was to take the total punishment of the men! Thirty-six lashes less one third! Nausea churned in her stomach and she struggled not to gag. She opened her mouth to scream at the deception, but a leather strip was shoved brutally between her teeth and strangled the outburst in her throat. Through wide tear-blurred eyes she could just make out the Colonel grinning over the passive squaw's shoulder whilst chewing his cigar and reaching around to squeeze her breasts. Belinda cursed her own pathetic naivety.

The Indian pressed his hand into her back, pushing her hard against the post. There was a long low whistle and Belinda's back erupted as the sound of the whip cracked across the small parade ground. When she opened her eyes she saw the wretched Colonel grinning smugly and gathering up the hem of the squaw's tunic. There was a pause, during which Belinda wondered how she could take another twenty-three of those horrendous blows. She would surely die. Tears welled up afresh as she realised she would die and nobody would care. They would probably just dump her in the wilderness where wild animals would dispose of her carcass. Her family would never know of her fate. The dam broke and she sobbed uncontrollably.

The whip hissed again and the tip curled around her buttocks and hips. She writhed against the post and her legs sagged. Her head lolled back and she hung limply, the twine cutting into her wrists.

The remaining strikes barely registered in her delirious mind, although her trussed body jerked like a puppet with each cruel sting of the whip.

When she slowly realised the punishment was over she peered through the gloom and bravely held the stare of the Colonel. He was pinching the squaw's now naked nipples, and her arm seemed to be moving rhythmically. As Belinda watched through a whirlpool of emotions the tip of his cigar flared orange as he drew deeply and then something glutinous and pale splattered up onto the window behind which they stood. Belinda felt sick as she realised how much her beating had stimulated the monster, and averted her eyes as yet more evidence of his excitement hit the glass. He wasn't fit to be in the army, let alone an officer in the army. Belinda spiralled into unconsciousness...

Captain Harding and Sergeant Riley carried the brave young lady to a small shack and laid her gently on some soft sacks of grain. Their respect for her was immense, and so they arranged for some elderly and wise squaw's to look after her. She slept for two whole days while the caring women constantly bathed her burning body with cool water and dribbled it between her parched lips. Special lotions helped sterilise and heal her wounds, and when her fever finally broke she found that the Colonel refused to see her and had forbidden his men to have any contact with her.

Chapter Twelve

Death Valley, in spite of its name and the terrifying tales Sheriff Hanglin had told, turned out to be perhaps the most straightforward part of Belinda's journey. This was partly due to the fact that it was not the hottest time of year, autumn having taken over from summer, but the principal saving factor was that, as Captain Harding had said, she was cutting across the very bottom of the notorious desert oven. The true tales of horror had arisen from those pioneers who had headed due west, towards the area that would become San Francisco. They had to cross the full width of the parched wasteland, and many died on the way. Their circumstances were aggravated by the agonisingly slow progress they made with their laden wagons, the extra days spent in the roasting heat eating into their limited supplies of water.

Even Belinda's far shorter southwesterly crossing had claimed many lives. She was able to find her way by simply following the skeletons of horses and cattle that littered the desert trail, with frequent simple graves by the wayside to remind her that she too was vulnerable.

She certainly suffered a great degree of misery and exhaustion, but at least she met no other person, a fact she was beginning to count as a blessing.

She now had a good horse and adequate water, along with some foul-tasting food called pemmican. These had been gifts from the troopers and the Indian who had whipped her, it having transpired that he was the father of the girl the fiendish Colonel had used as additional spice whilst watching Belinda's punishment. She had been alarmed when the Captain, Sergeant, troopers and Indian had surreptitiously visited the shed where she had lain recovering for three days. Alarmed because one of the troopers had grinned and said 'We just had a whip round for you', but her obvious fear was quickly quelled by the Captain explaining that the term meant they had held a collection amongst themselves to pay for a saddle and harness and a set of suitable clothing from the fort's trading post. The fine horse itself was a gift from the Indian, and he had personally escorted her away from the fort to set her in the right direction.

'Are you sure you don't want anything for the horse?' she had repeatedly asked him, but he had been adamant that it was a gift. She had no money but still felt duty-bound to at least enquire as a means of expressing her appreciation. In fact, her covert glances at the tantalising protrusion in the front of his buckskins had her wishing he would extract some form of payment from her.

He finally left her and headed back to the fort. Her desire to cross the desert and get to Los Angeles drove her to ride for as many hours of the day and night as she could. This not only meant she covered the distance more quickly and helped her water supply go further, but it also reduced the time she had to spend sleeping on the ground; she had seen enough rattlesnakes as she rode along to find it a terrifying prospect every time she descended from the horse. She even deferred her toiletries as long as possible due to her dread of squatting defenceless and bare-bottomed over that hellish sand.

After a few days of this unpleasant terrain the sand started to mingle with clay and weeds and, at last, she was relieved and overjoyed to see a couple of spindly trees on a small hill about a mile to her left. With a hand shielding her eyes from the relentless sun and squinting through the rising heat haze she was overjoyed to discern what looked like a white church on that same hill. She spurred the horse forward with a dig of her heels and diverted from the main trail to seek help or comfort from that sanctuary.

The building was in the Spanish style, with a cross mounted on top of the bell tower. There was a well, similarly white, in front of large studded double doors. Elated at the prospect of some fresh water, Belinda dismounted and wound the handle until a full bucket appeared. Just the sound of the clear liquid slopping over the bucket's sides cooled her blood. She drank deeply, and then emptied the remainder into a trough for the horse.

Feeling invigorated she studied the silent building as it shimmered in the afternoon heat, and saw an inscription across the arched door. *Convent of the Sisters of Little Mercy*, it read in English. She was pleased to know it was a proper religious establishment, rather than something weird like the Danish sect, and she smiled at the name. Presumably it had been incorrectly translated from the Spanish and should have read *Convent of the Little Sisters of Mercy*. She was just wondering if it was in fact occupied when a small door set into the main portal opened and out stepped a smiling nun.

Slightly built, she looked sweet and peaceful in her black habit, and the face that beamed from the head covering was gentle and caring. She beckoned to Belinda, who tethered the horse by the trough and approached.

'Please enter,' said the nun sweetly. 'Someone will care for your horse shortly.'

As Belinda passed through the solid door she was surprised to find so much light inside, due to the building being constructed around an open central courtyard with a latticed roof to help cool the heat of the day. There were cloisters around the perimeter and various rooms between the cloisters and the main walls. The room at the far end appeared to be the chapel itself as it was larger than the rest and was ornately decorated. Belinda noticed there was a distinct lack of religious symbols, but thought little of it. An enormously long table took up a lot of the stone-flagged courtyard, and there were many other nuns at work there. Some were scrubbing the floor, some were preparing vegetables at the table, and others were sewing or washing clothes. They whispered quietly to each other, and an atmosphere of peace and tranquillity pervaded the scene. For a second Belinda thought that if it were not for her family commitments she could have happily ended her journey right there.

The nuns appeared not to notice her arrival, until her escort addressed them in a crystal clear voice.

'Sisters, we have a visitor.'

At that they all stopped what they were doing and excitedly gathered around Belinda. They were all of about her age and beautiful, but again Belinda saw little significance in this. She was amused rather than alarmed when they started stroking her body and hair with murmurs of admiration. They felt the silky blouse and the rich wool of her long skirt, and whilst there was nothing improper in their attentions, Belinda was more than a little flustered to find that the situation and the gentle contact was beginning to arouse her. She would not have felt so much at ease had they been men, of course. But they were all very sweet and gentle, and Belinda felt relaxed and at peace.

Suddenly the cooing and touching stopped as an imperious voice boomed, 'I see we have been blessed with a guest.'

All the nuns turned and looked towards the chapel, where a large and older nun stood. She too was dressed in the same traditional black and white habit, but her higher rank was symbolised by a string of large rosary beads hanging around her neck and an enormous starched headpiece that projected in every direction. Belinda detected that the other nuns held her in a high degree of awe.

'You are called?' she asked Belinda, with a hint of a Spanish accent within a voice that was rich and deep.

'No, no,' Belinda replied hurriedly. 'I've just crossed the desert and I hoped I might be allowed some rest and shelter here before moving on. My horse and I are quite exhausted.'

The gathered nuns giggled like excitable schoolgirls at this silly answer.

'No, my child,' said the dominant nun. 'I meant, what are you called? What is your name?'

Belinda blushed deeply with embarrassment at her mistake as she told her.

'Do you wish to sojourn with us a while, Belinda?' the nun enquired.

'Yes please, sister,' she replied meekly, a little overawed by the woman's presence.

There was a gasp from the nuns and one of them whispered sharply to Belinda, 'Salmacis! The name is Salmacis!'

Belinda's blush went from crimson to purple. 'Sorry – Salmacis,' she corrected the error in little more than a whisper. 'I didn't know that was your name.'

'Do not worry child,' smiled the nun called Salmacis. 'We all make mistakes from time to time.

187

That is, after all, why most of us are here.' She clapped her hands sharply. 'Sister Maria! Sister Dolores! Show our guest to a cell and make her feel at home. I will speak with you later, Belinda.'

The nun who had brought her into the convent and another one-stepped forward as the others drifted away, some with barely concealed disappointment. Obviously it would have been more fun to settle a visitor in than return to their chores.

As Salmacis swept away into another room beside the chapel Sisters Maria and Dolores guided Belinda to a small side room, which was indeed a cell. It was windowless and bare, with just a single narrow bed of rough wood covered with a thin blanket. The only light filtered from the central courtyard via a small barred window set in the door.

Once the door was closed the two nuns surprised Belinda by giggling and tickling her under the arms and on the back of the neck. In the half-light Belinda laughed at such good-natured fun, and didn't resist when the banter resulted in her being pushed down until she was lying back on the bed. The skirt rucked-up and nimble fingers raced over her stomach and up and down her legs from booted ankle to knee. Belinda, not too sure about all this but wanting to be polite, tried to tickle them in return but they were too fast for her and kept skipping back out of range. After a few minutes she stopped trying and simply lay on her back smiling up at the sisters. The three of them were slightly out of breath, and a strange electricity suddenly filled the tiny room. The laughter subsided and the smiles faded. Each of them knew what was to happen next. Sisters Maria and Dolores moved in close again, but this time their twinkling eyes had a glint of desire and intent in them. It was a look that Belinda recognised, but instead of being alarmed she found her heart thumping with suppressed excitement. The two nuns knelt beside the bed as though preparing to pray.

She did not resist when the resumed tickles turned to sensual caresses on her legs. As before, they worked their way beneath the skirt from her ankles to her knees, but this time they continued their journey as they intently watched her for any reaction. Sister Dolores eased Belinda's thighs apart and then cupped her vulva in her cool palm. She smiled slightly at Belinda's tiny gasp of pleasure, and pressed a little harder. At the same time Sister Maria undid Belinda's blouse and slipped her hands inside the silk to squeeze both her breasts. Though totally taken aback at this unexpected development Belinda smiled her sheepish encouragement, and urged her aching breasts up into the waiting hands. She suddenly stiffened and sighed, and Sister Maria licked her lips and watched avidly as her colleague's hidden hands started to work beneath the skirt.

Just as Belinda was beginning to think she was about to embarrass herself by coming in front of two such devout young ladies, the hands between her legs disappeared. She could not deny her deep disappointment. But they quickly returned at the hem of the skirt and began to fold it back. First her shapely calves were exposed, then her perfect thighs, and then the skirt was raised above her waist to show her full glory; her gentle fold peeping from its nest of chestnut hair. All three females sighed heavily as Maria bent to suck Belinda's nearest nipple into her mouth and Dolores stroked the damp chestnut curls with a strong middle finger. Once again Belinda soared towards her orgasm, and once again she was denied as the two nuns released her and swapped places. Dolores rolled

Belinda's nipples between her fingers and thumbs whilst Maria bent low again to run the tip of her tongue up and down between Belinda's sex-lips until she was writhing ecstatically on the bed. She was loving the gentle female attention. Men had the advantage of possessing penises, but they all seemed to be so cruel. Some women were cruel too, she reminded herself, but nonetheless there was a tenderness about females in general that was appealing to her more and more.

Once again, and when she was least expecting it, the hands and mouth left her and the two nuns straightened up. They both gripped their habits and raised their eyebrows.

'Yes…' pleaded Belinda softly in answer to their silent question. 'Please…' She could not resist touching herself between her thighs as the habits slowly rustled higher and higher. Their thighs were like porcelain, and the tension had Belinda breathing deeply as the black garments approached crotch level. Feeling almost faint with excitement she held her orgasm back, ready to let it explode as soon as the erotic vision of the nuns' vaginas came into view.

To Belinda's eternal shame the only explosion that did come was caused by the cell door crashing open to reveal, framed in the doorway, a furious-looking Salmacis.

That evening at sunset the mortified Belinda was taken from her cell and delivered to Salmacis. The austere nun was sitting on a wooden throne in the room next to the chapel, which appeared to be there for private worship. Sisters Maria and Dolores were standing at each side of the throne, their heads bowed in shame.

'You may leave us,' Salmacis said to the nun who

190

had collected Belinda. The door closed and the domineering nun sat studying Belinda for a long and unsettling period. 'Are you ashamed of yourself, Belinda Hopeworth?' she finally asked.

'Why should I be?' replied Belinda defiantly.

'Because you enter our home,' her tone was strong but calm, 'and within minutes you are frolicking with two of my sisters.'

'They started it.'

Sister Maria looked up. 'That is not true, dear Salmacis—'

'Silence!' snapped the nun, raising her hands. 'I will not have such bickering in my house!'

Belinda had nothing further to say. She fiddled uncomfortably with the front of her skirt.

'Kneel,' ordered Salmacis with undeniable authority. Belinda was about to ask why she should do anything she was told, when she decided it would probably be better to appease her quickly and then get away as soon as she was able. She knelt just in front of the nun's knees with her head bowed. From beneath her eyelashes she saw the knees part. 'Come closer...' she heard. She hesitated a moment, and then shuffled forward until surprisingly sturdy thighs gripped her sides. Her breasts squashed against the seat of the throne and hands lay her head on the lap against which she was tightly pinned.

'You know you must be punished for your wantonness, don't you?' came the rich voice. So should the two nuns, thought Belinda, they started it all. She tried to respond but the hands held her head firmly, and when they sensed her resistance subsiding they gently stroked her hair. 'It is for your own good.' The voice was almost hypnotic. Belinda breathed deeply and relaxed. She sensed movement, and then

191

felt her skirt being raised. The still air was cool on her thighs and bottom. She knew what to expect, and clenched Salmacis' habit in readiness.

With the first blow she jerked forward and her breasts squashed into the apex of Salmacis' thighs. What had hit her she knew not, but the pain was terrible. The second strike dragged a scream from her lungs. From their rapid delivery she guessed that both nuns were beating her with individual implements. Tears sprung from her tightly clenched eyes and dampened the habit beneath her flushed cheek. The blows continued, and all the time the hands caressed her hair. The bizarre contrast between affection and brutality made her emotions spin. She gripped the habit even tighter in her fists until the colour drained from her knuckles.

Gradually, through waves of conflicting emotions, Belinda became aware of a tiny swelling beneath her cheek. What it could be she had no idea, but the size and pressure was definitely increasing steadily. So distracted was she by it that she did not realise the punishment had ceased until she heard Salmacis dismiss the two nuns in a tone charged with emotion. The door opened and closed for the second time, and the room was left still and quiet.

'Belinda,' Salmacis whispered, 'we are alone.' The pressure of the thighs increased and the hands left her hair. 'We have a few moments together before I must take evening chapel.'

Belinda didn't know what to expect next, and decided it would be safest to remain curled up and quiet. The heat from the lump beneath the habit was getting stronger against her face. She became aware of the black habit being tugged up.

'Although you are a promiscuous sinner,' continued

Salmacis, 'I will allow you to rest in my house for tonight.' The habit inched higher. 'But I expect you to be gone by first light.'

'Thank you,' whispered Belinda into the dense fabric.

'And in return you will now show your gratitude. I have little time, so make haste.'

'But what do you want of me?'

Suddenly the habit was tugged away and a relatively small but stiffly erect penis sprang against her lips. Belinda shrieked with horror, but a hand instantly clamped over her mouth to silence her. As she relaxed slightly the hand cautiously released its hold, but the hairy thighs maintained their embrace.

'Do not be alarmed!' hissed the freak as he cupped her cheeks and stared into her wide eyes. 'Yes – I am a man! And because I need to dress as a woman I have been pilloried and run out of more towns than you could ever imagine!'

Belinda couldn't speak. Never before in her life had she seen or heard of such a thing.

'My nuns know what I am – and they still love me.' Once Salmacis could see she wasn't going to scream or struggle he continued. 'I see in your eyes great compassion, Belinda.' One hand slipped furtively to the back of her head and pressed so gently she barely noticed. 'I sensed it the instant I first set eyes on you. Do not forsake me out of ignorance. Do not forsake me like all the others.' As Belinda continued to stare confusedly up into the hypnotic eyes the other hand gripped the base of the rigid cock and aimed it at her slightly parted lips. 'Do not reject me, Belinda…'

The pressure increased further and Belinda's astonished face sank until her nose nestled in thick curly hair. Her mouth was filled with stiff flesh and his

193

male musk invaded her nostrils.

'That feels good, child,' croaked Salmacis as he lifted and lowered her head. 'Use your feminine magic on me. Prove to me your compassion – time is short.'

Utterly bewildered, Belinda sucked and licked instinctively. The room was now filled with her wet sounds and his heavy panting. Her face was lifted and lowered time and time again. Her lips slid tightly up and down the shaft, and little pools of saliva dribbled down to his balls.

From next door came the muted sounds of the young nuns gathering in the chapel for evening service.

'You are doing well, child… you will soon be rewarded.' With that he pushed her back onto her haunches and grappled frantically with the buttons of her blouse. She knelt without emotion as he tugged and pulled at her. When open he ripped the blouse free from her skirt, pulled her forward roughly, and moulded her perspiring breasts around his standing erection. 'Now…' he hissed, his bloodshot eyes bulging demonically. 'Here comes your reward for having faith in me… I shall anoint you.' He stabbed his hips at her a few times and then spat his seed into her cleavage. A second barrage spattered her throat and chin, from where it dripped back onto her sensitive breasts. His thighs almost squeezed the very breath from her lungs as he arched and quelled a scream of undiluted passion. Belinda knelt, unmoving and devoid of feeling, as he used his deflating penis to smooth his cream over her breasts and nipples.

Gradually Salmacis subsided into the throne and regained his composure. He arrogantly wiped his small penis on her silk blouse and straightened his habit as though nothing had happened between them at all.

'Very good. You may return to your cell. You will find soap and water and food there.' He grinned sardonically. 'Never let it be said that we at the Convent of the Sisters of Little Mercy are not hospitable.' Belinda stood and walked to the door without a word. As she opened it Salmacis casually called after her, 'Remember, you are to be gone before first light. And if you tell any one of what has gone this evening I will know and will personally hunt you down and kill you.'

Chapter Thirteen

Belinda was drowning, caught in a fast current flowing between sheer rock walls, just thirty minutes after leaving the irregular convent.

She had emerged into the approaching dawn unhindered by any of the nuns, and was annoyed to see that her horse was still where she had tethered it by the well, in spite of the nun's promise that someone would attend to it. She picked up a dry rock and hurled it at the white wall in anger and frustration. It crumbled ineffectively into dust upon impact.

Using the rising sun as a navigational aid, she had found that she did not need to return to the main trail that she had followed across Death Valley, but could continue her journey by following the track alongside a river gorge. She knew she needed to be on the other side of that tight ravine, and was pleased to see a small bridge just ahead.

Halfway across the span, with the foaming water flowing briskly twenty feet below, the horse suddenly whinnied and reared up. Belinda too gave a shriek as she saw a coiled snake immediately ahead, its head raised and its hideous rattle vibrating threateningly. The panic-stricken horse tried to turn on the tight bridge as it reared, and before she could react Belinda found herself sliding off its back over the parapet and into the torrent below.

Now she cursed the heavy riding skirt as its weight kept dragging her down every time she fought her way to the surface to gulp some air. Her boots didn't help either, and the confusion and spinning of her body made it impossible for her to get rid of those hindrances.

She knew she was finally about to die when she felt an iron-like hand thrust between her thighs and grip her crotch. Another clamped onto her left breast and twisted agonisingly. They could not be real, just a deadly delirium caused by lack of air and too much water, and she emitted a terrified sob. Even in her last moments her imagination was subjecting her to one final abuse. Just as she prepared to release her slim grasp on life itself she was hauled to the surface and dragged against the side of a large canoe. The hands adjusted their position and supported her under the arms, and she looked up into the beaming face of a giant with a mass of shocking red hair. The freezing water swamped her again and she fought to breathe as an identical but slightly smaller giant joined the other and beamed down, before they effortlessly dragged her over the side of the vessel and spilled her into the bottom. She lay coughing and spluttering for some time, gasping to fill her burning lungs and not daring to believe that she had really been saved.

'Howdy!' shouted the bigger redhead over the roar of the river with a broad grin as if it was all one jolly game. 'Glad you could join us!'

Belinda crouched low, her shoulders and breasts heaving and her soaking clothes stuck to her like a second skin. The couple grabbed their oars and soon had control of the canoe again as it raced and pitched along with the flow.

'My horse!' she suddenly blurted. 'Did my horse get away?' She looked up at the larger of the two redheads, paddling from the rear of the canoe, and realised it was a woman!

'Don't you worry yourself, honey!' the female mountain bellowed back. 'Skedaddled soon as you hit the water!'

That news cheered Belinda a little. Very slowly her breathing calmed and she began to feel better. Despite the wet clothing she was warmed by the rising sun. She knelt up and watched her two saviours navigate the small craft with fascinating ease and skill through the maze of treacherous and slime-covered rocks jutting out of the roaring torrent. 'Thank you for saving me!' she shouted, but the woman just grinned and said nothing.

A few miles further downstream the river widened out and calmed considerably. They drifted on in the morning sun, boosted occasionally as the paddles dipped into the refreshing looking water. They were towing a second canoe that was piled high with furs. Here it was easy to communicate without shouting.

'Where are you going?' asked Belinda.

'Down river,' said the female trapper. As yet the man had not uttered a sound.

'Anywhere near a place called Los Angeles?' asked Belinda, without any real hope.

'Yep,' said the woman, and then she spat lazily into the river as Belinda's face brightened. 'We stay with this ditch as far as the sea at Pedra Bay. Los Angeles is a few miles north of there, maybe a day's walk. Don't know what you want to go there for though, goddam no-hope dump.' The tough but handsomely attractive female saw her studying the cargo canoe. 'Yep, honey, we're trappers, me and that dumb-ass who calls himself my brother.' The man at the front gave a high-pitched and almost childlike giggle without taking his eyes from the river ahead. 'Our fur gets sent to the finest cities all over Europe,' added the female. 'Worn by all the rich, it is.'

Belinda had nothing to say, so she just watched the

water gently lapping against the side of the canoe and allowed it to soothe her further – excited by the thought that she was almost at her goal. She tried to imagine what her Uncle Albert might look like, and smiled at the idea that he was at that very moment going about his daily affairs completely oblivious of the fact that his niece from Liverpool in England was about to drop in on him. The smile widened as she imagined the joy at the meeting and saw herself being warmly welcomed by his homely wife and excited children.

'My name's Hannah,' the female interrupted her happy reverie. 'And that great lump there,' she nodded forward at her brother, 'is Hank.' He giggled again. It seemed everything his sister said was funny.

'Belinda,' she smiled. 'My name's Belinda.'

Silence fell over the canoe again, broken only by the surrounding sounds of nature and the occasional dip of the paddle breaking the surface of the clear water.

After a short while the two turned the vessels into a small grassy cove. In no time Hannah had collected driftwood and built and lit a fire on the bank while Hank waded around hunting fish. His stealth for a big man was surprising, and Belinda watched him for a while with fascination.

'Best get those damp clothes off you before you catch a chill,' said Hannah once she was happy the fire had established itself and had hung a pot of coffee over it. Belinda wrapped her arms around herself bashfully.

'Oh, I think I'm all right. They're nearly dry now.'

'Don't be silly,' said Hannah, standing. 'Last thing you want is to get a fever way out here.' She scanned their surroundings in a way that made Belinda shiver. 'I've seen folk a lot tougher than you die in hours for not paying this land enough respect.'

Belinda checked to see where Hank was; he had waded around a piece of jutting rock. 'Well... perhaps you're right.' She gingerly undid the top button of her blouse. 'But I have nothing to wear while they're drying.'

'No problem,' smiled Hannah. 'We got a canoe full of furs to hide your blushes and keep you warm.' She stepped close to Belinda, who would have backed away had it not been for Hannah gently but firmly gripping her wrists. At this close proximity her odour was quite overpowering. 'Here,' said the big woman, 'let me.'

'Th-thank you,' stammered Belinda, 'but I can manage.'

'I said, let me.'

Belinda fell silent and allowed her hands to be pulled down to her sides. She knew it was pointless to argue.

Hannah stared with little expression as each button popped and more and more of the shadowy cleavage was revealed to her. When all the buttons were undone she left the blouse tucked into the skirt and slipped it off Belinda's smooth shoulders. Her calloused hands rubbed Belinda's sensitive flesh as they moved down her arms. Both females remained silent. The blouse was lowered until it gathered around Belinda's elbows, and there Hannah left it. Belinda's movements were restricted, and her firm damp breasts were exposed to Hannah's lusty gaze and desires.

'I think Hank's taken a liking to you,' Hannah said as her great hands reached slowly up for Belinda's breasts. Her face lowered and her lips pressed against Belinda's. Belinda gasped into the mouth as her breasts were cupped and weighed. A wet tongue wormed into her mouth. Fingers pinched her nipples.

Belinda was dumbstruck; was everybody in this country wandering around in a permanent state of sexual arousal looking for someone to seduce? At the same time her spinning thoughts were trying to fathom how Hannah had come to such a conclusion about her brother; he had barely looked at Belinda, and had certainly not spoken to her.

'Can't say as I blame him,' panted Hannah as she broke away from the kiss. Belinda blushed at the unusual compliment. 'You know,' Hannah persisted, 'there's nothing I enjoy better than a good-looking young lass. But being stuck out here in the wilderness for so long it's been quite a while since I had me one, know what I mean?'

Belinda knew she had to put a stop to this folly. 'I'm sorry, Hannah, I'd like you to let go of me,' she said bravely. 'I don't feel the same way.'

Hannah flicked the sweetly erect nipples she held and Belinda instinctively sighed. 'Is that right, now?' she mocked knowingly. Belinda silently cursed her own traitorous body.

Hank had returned from his hunt and stood dripping from the waist down and holding four glistening fish. He giggled at the alluring sight of his sister stroking the young lady's naked breasts.

'Hank,' Hannah addressed him without averting her gaze from Belinda's breasts. 'Young missy here seems to think she's entitled to free passage down river, free food, and free coffee.'

Hank giggled.

'No,' said Belinda hastily. 'I'll gladly pay you once I get to Los Angeles. I'll forward some money to wherever you want it.'

'And we're supposed to trust you, are we?' sneered Hannah.

'You have my word.'

'Word don't mean shit,' said Hannah, and spat again. Hank giggled.

'Why are you being so horrible to me?' whispered Belinda, the continuing stimulation of her nipples making her moist between her legs.

'We're not being horrible, honey,' mocked Hannah. 'We could leave you out here where nobody would ever find you. Now that would be horrible.'

Hank seemed to like that idea.

Belinda was shocked at the veiled threat. 'You wouldn't,' she stammered.

'We might,' confirmed Hannah. 'Don't take it personal, honey – this is business, is all. We're not a charity. We always believe in getting payment in one shape or form up front. Have you any money on you at all?'

Belinda shook her head.

'Well,' sighed Hannah. 'It's up to you. You can come with us, be safe, and eat our food… or you can stay out here with all the savages and wild animals and poisonous snakes and fend for yourself. We'll leave you to make up your mind.'

With that Hannah and Hank left Belinda standing alone. Hank stripped off his soaked buckskins, without any modesty whatsoever, and squatted down with his sister. Belinda felt her cheeks flush at the sight of his nudity and coyly averted her eyes as they cleaned the fish with large broad-bladed knives, and skewered them over the fire. Soon the mouth-watering aromas of coffee and cooking fish wafted into the air on the blue/grey smoke that seemed to drift under Belinda's nose with uncanny accuracy. The two trappers talked quietly and casually together as though Belinda wasn't there, while her stomach gurgled with hunger.

Belinda got the message, but wondered sadly why everyone in America seemed to want to take advantage of her as soon as set eyes on her. Was she a wicked temptress as Rachel had said? Was it all her fault?

While she was deep in self-recriminatory thought Hank cooked up a pot of bean stew to go with the fish, and her wavering resolve was broken. She reached the decision which was never really in any serious doubt; she would consent to their demands – if only to bring her nightmare journey to a quicker conclusion.

'Very well,' she said. The brother and sister didn't respond, but kept talking to each other. Belinda felt humiliated; they were playing games and making her beg for her own seduction. 'I said very well,' she repeated a little louder. 'I'll do anything you want.' This time they looked up at her and smiled. They slopped the food onto three metal plates and signalled for Belinda to sit on the ground beside them. For the next ten minutes the threesome ate in silence. Belinda could not believe how matter-of-fact they were; she had just offered herself for them to do with as they wished, and yet they preferred to eat at their leisure first. During the meal Belinda didn't know where to look; every time she raised her eyes they seemed to fall upon the soft but large penis sprouting from Hank's ginger thatch. Hannah watched her embarrassment with amusement.

'Time for a wash,' said Hannah when all three plates had been scraped clean and the coffee drunk. 'Get your clothes off, honey.' Hank took off his shirt and Hannah stripped. They were both lean, and Belinda watched their muscles ripple impressively as they ran and splashed noisily into the river. Feeling less self-conscious without them watching her Belinda did the same and joined them, quickly submerging herself before they could witness her nudity. The refreshing water made her feel good, and soon she was shrieking and laughing with the trappers as they relaxed and enjoyed themselves. Hannah and Hank wrestled playfully, and when Belinda floated within reach they quickly grabbed her and included her in the mock fight. Beneath the surface hands fumbled and pinched and poked. It all seemed quite innocent, but gradually the laughter subsided and the hands began to stroke and tease. Belinda found herself enjoying the intimate touches, and allowed the brother and sister to take liberties without complaint. Something large and soft slapped against her bottom and her insides churned with excitement. Hannah held her and their wet slippery breasts squashed together. They kissed deeply and Belinda felt the stalk stiffening against the small of her back as Hank pressed close in behind. Hannah lowered herself into the water, flipped Belinda over so that her head lay between her muscular breasts, and then lifted the passive girl until she floated with her bobbing breasts just breaking the gently flowing surface. The sun warmed her face and budding nipples. Her wet hair lay shining on Hannah's pale skin. Hank slithered in between Belinda's legs, his now fully erect penis swaying on top of the water like a serpent. His fingers rummaged between her thighs and peeled her open. Belinda used her arms to help her float, and then closed her eyes as Hank's engorged helmet nudged past his fingers and entered her. Her breasts rose higher and rivulets of water glistened in the morning sun. A pool of clear water gathered in her hollowed stomach as she breathed deeply. Huge strong hands cupped her buttocks and slowly eased her back and forth. Hannah whispered encouragement to her brother. He giggled with delight, looking down at the young beauty impaled on his length. His thick ginger thatch meshed with her glossy chestnut curls. The surrounding water began to chop up as he slid her up and down his length like a weightless doll. Belinda rolled her head on Hannah's chest, and then before she realised it was coming her orgasm overwhelmed her and she whimpered in ecstasy. At the same moment Hank's face contorted. He withdrew from the gasping girl and squirted his seed into the sparkling pool on her trembling stomach. His hips jerked again and another volley arched through the air and splattered onto her vulnerable breasts.

Back on the grassy bank in the shade of a tree Belinda lay replete while Hannah kissed her all over. The strong woman made love to her with surprising tenderness, and then lay back herself while Belinda worked hard to make her come. Afterwards Hank used Belinda's mouth while she writhed over Hannah's face. At the moment of truth he withdrew again and came on her breasts. Belinda loved every moment, and began to feel growing affection towards the brother and sister.

The next few days were an erotic blur for Belinda. Had her circumstances been any different she would have happily stayed with Hannah and Hank for as long as they would have her along.

Soon it was their last evening together. They would be reaching the tiny trading port of Pedra Bay late the next day. Hannah and Hank would unload and sell their skins, get blind drunk, pick up a woman or two, and then start their extremely arduous journey back upstream. And Belinda would set off on the last tiny leg of her odyssey.

Belinda felt immense gratitude towards them both. They had brought her safely to within touching distance of her goal, and had shown her more kindness than anybody since Tom McLaren. By way of a thank you she made languid love to Hank in front of the campfire, sitting astride his standing erection and cupping his huge hands in her own as they massaged her breasts. Then she crouched between Hannah's thighs and kissed and licked her to a thunderous orgasm whilst allowing the quickly revitalised Hank to penetrate her bottom and come for the final time in that private place.

Chapter Fourteen

Having left Hannah and Hank at the tiny saloon in Pedra Bay in a raucous and drunken stupor, Belinda found a barn on the edge of the hamlet and slept uncomfortably until dawn. In the cool light she set off north with the Pacific Ocean crashing on her left and mountains shimmering distantly on her right. The road sometimes hugged the beach, where she stripped and had an early dip, whilst at other times it wandered inland and became alarmingly desert-like.

A Mexican family with a donkey and cart gave her a lift for a couple of hours. The man and his wife sat up front and Belinda had to squash in with their five teenage sons, chastely ignoring their amorous and lurid expressions. She was too tired and too excited to care about anything except that within a matter of hours she would have finally reached her uncle's town.

After the family dropped her off she walked on with ever-increasing spirits. She did, however, have one alarming encounter just around midday when she was surprised to stumble across a group of drunken hobos. They started pestering her and begging for money. Their filthy hands were unnecessarily familiar with her charms, and she found herself being pushed from one to the other as they crowded around. It was obvious they were not going to accept no for an answer until, almost in tears, she begged them to leave her in peace. She said she wasn't bothering anyone and simply wanted to get to her uncle, Albert Hopeworth, in Los Angeles. It was as if she had said something magical. The men withdrew at once, humbly doffing their hats, bowing respectfully, apologising profusely and blaming each other for having taken such liberties.

Belinda was highly impressed at the effect her uncle's name had on them. He was clearly a highly respected man in a position of considerable rank and therefore, she assumed, wealthy as well. He would almost certainly have enough money to arrange her passage back to England, or, since she had set out to emigrate anyway, to establish her in some honest money earning capacity. It was perfectly reasonable to think there might be a shortage of music teachers in this part of the world. As the rabble backed away, mumbling and cursing each other's stupidity, she clapped her hands in glee and hurried on, her tiredness suddenly forgotten.

She had not come to Los Angeles in search of excitement, so she felt no disappointment as she gazed down on the small town, dominated by a large church at the highest point. It looked a very sedate sort of place from her vantage point, which was exactly what she wanted. She had had quite enough excitement in the last few months – enough to last her a lifetime.

She could scarcely believe she had finally reached journey's end as she walked downhill and into the town's choking dust. Her uncle would never be able to appreciate how much she had suffered in reaching him, because she would never be able to tell him. She would have to make up some white lies, making out that everyone had been very kind and had helped her make the journey without her ever once having to spend any money. She knew it sounded pretty unbelievable, but it was the best she could come up with.

The town's streets were deserted and all of the buildings closed up as if no one lived there. She wandered around for a while and at last saw an old man on a donkey, but when she asked him if he knew how she might find her uncle he just hurried past muttering.

The main street widened after a few hundred yards and there was a definite shopping centre, though all of these premises were shut too. At least Belinda could see by their window displays that they were in business, and then wondered if everybody was having one of those siestas of which she'd heard.

She peered curiously through the window of the nearest shop, and was cheered to see a young lady in the dusky interior – but then realised she was crying. The young lady stopped when she saw Belinda looking in, and dried her eyes with a lace hanky. Once she had touched her hair into place and checked her appearance in a hand glass she approached and unbolted and opened the door.

She was a pretty girl of about eighteen years, and her delicate floral dress highlighted her slender nubility. 'We're closed,' she said sweetly. 'I'm afraid you'll have to come back later.'

'No, you don't understand,' Belinda blurted hastily to prevent the door from being closed in her face. 'I was wondering if you can help me.'

'I'm sorry – I don't think so,' she replied and made to close the door.

'Please,' begged Belinda. 'If I could just come in for a moment and explain.'

The girl looked nervously over her shoulder and chewed her lip while she pondered this for a few seconds. 'Very well,' she said at last. 'But keep your voice down – and be quick.' She stood aside and glanced up and down the street as Belinda stepped into the gloomy leather shop. After the glare from outside it took some time for her eyes to fully adjust to the new

209

environment. The girl re-bolted the door and lowered the blinds.

'What is troubling you?' asked Belinda with genuine concern. Her problems were almost over, so her own need for assistance could wait. This pretty girl was in more distress than she.

'I cannot tell you,' she sniffled.

Belinda held her hands in her own, feeling sudden pity and affection for the poor girl. 'Tell me – I may be able to help.'

'You cannot.'

'Try – it'll help you just to talk to someone.'

'My…'

'Yes… tell me,' she prompted gently.

The girl took a deep breath. 'My guardian… he's going to beat me,' she blurted miserably.

'Why?' asked Belinda, squeezing her hands reassuringly. 'What have you done?'

'Nothing,' she looked at Belinda with clear blue eyes. Her chin quivered slightly. 'The till was down a cent this morning. He says it was my fault, but I know it was him. He's always making mistakes, whereas I'm very good with sums.'

'Then you must tell him,' advised Belinda.

'I daren't – you don't know him. He's a very strict man. He'd beat me all the more if I spoke against him.' She lowered her gaze and continued softly. 'And besides – he's a good man really. He takes care of me. He keeps me safe… as long as I am obedient and nice to him.'

Belinda suspected as much.

'He'll be down in a minute.' An idea clearly came to the girl and she brightened hopefully. 'Perhaps you could speak with him on my behalf?'

Belinda's heart went out to the lovely girl. 'Of

course I will,' she said warmly. 'Do you think he'll listen to me, though?'

'Oh, I'm sure he will...' said the girl joyously, 'because you are so beautiful.'

Belinda didn't quite see why that should make any difference as to whether he punished his charge or not, but decided not to dampen the girl's renewed spirits by raising such trivia. 'Tell me,' she said. 'Why do you have a guardian in the first place? Where are your parents?'

The girl looked a little sad again and Belinda immediately cursed herself for being so tactless. 'My mother and father are both dead,' she whispered.

Belinda could have ripped out her tongue and fed it to the strays out in the streets. 'Oh – I'm so sorry... I didn't mean—'

'It's all right,' smiled the girl bravely. 'It happened when I was very young. I barely remember them. The court made me a ward of my guardian and his wife because they were close friends of my parents and they had this good business.'

'And has he always been strict?'

She nodded. 'Ever since I can remember. But it got worse a couple of years ago when his wife died. He suddenly got much more angry, and started paying a lot of attention towards me.'

'What sort of attention?' asked Belinda, although she had a pretty good idea.

She blushed. 'I would rather not say.'

Belinda took the girl in her arms and comforted her. Her hair smelt clean and fresh. Their curves moulded nicely together and Belinda felt a pang of guilt as she experienced a warm tingle in the pit of her stomach. She gasped slightly as a thigh innocently slipped between her own. 'What...' her voice trembled slightly, so she paused to delicately clear her throat. 'What is your name?'

'Sally,' whispered the compliant girl. Belinda reciprocated and affectionately kissed the silky hair at Sally's temple to reassure her. She lightly kissed across her forehead, and then her fluttering eyelids. She kissed the tip of her cute nose, and then they stared deeply at each other. Time stood still, and then their flushed faces moved closer – inch by breathtaking inch. Their full moist lips parted in readiness of the inevitable kiss. Belinda knew it was folly to allow it to go any further, but she really didn't care...

'Well, well, well,' a whiny voice broke the beautiful spell. Belinda and Sally sprang apart, coughing and smoothing down their clothing. Sally, doing the first thing that came into her head, snatched a feather duster and turned to the window display, while Belinda looked up at the source of the interruption. A man stood on the wooden stairs in the rear corner, his booted feet and trousers in view, his top half obscured by shadow. 'What have we here then?'

Step by step he descended until he stood at the bottom of the stairs. He was a thin lizard of a man, and his beady eyes quickly inspected the gorgeous newcomer. 'So,' he smiled crookedly, 'you have a visitor, Sally.' The smarmy way in which he licked his thin lips made Belinda shudder. 'And a very lovely visitor – if I may say so.'

'Yes sir,' Sally said nervously, without taking her eyes or the duster from the already dust free merchandise. Belinda had to admit that she felt uneasy in the presence of the slimy man, but now that her life was so close to being complete she had to stay and do what she could to help Sally.

212

'Well, my dearest Sally, I am sure you have enjoyed seeing your friend,' his eyes rose slowly from Belinda's feet to her breasts for the second time, and she knew that he had definitely enjoyed seeing her. 'But you must tell her it is now time to leave. You know very well that we have a little unfinished business to attend to.'

'Yes sir,' blustered Sally. 'Sorry sir.'

Belinda summoned her resolve. 'Actually, Mr…?' she began, but he didn't offer his name, leaving her in an awkward pause. 'Actually sir,' she began again, 'that's what I'd like to talk to you about. I don't think such a sweet girl should be punished so cruelly—'

'Oh you don't, don't you?'

'No sir, and I'd like to enter a plea on her behalf—'

'Oh you would, would you?'

'Yes, sir, I—'

His lip curled and Belinda fell silent, wondering at her wisdom in getting involved; it wasn't really her business, after all.

'It's all right, Belinda,' said Sally moving towards the door. 'I should not have asked for your help. I'll be just fine.'

'No wait,' said the man, holding up his hand and slithering across to them both. 'Perhaps I was a little hasty. Perhaps…' he openly gawped at Belinda's breasts.

'Belinda,' prompted Sally.

'Yes, quite…' his tongue darted across his lips, and Belinda half-expected it to be forked. 'Perhaps – Belinda – would like to suggest an alternative.'

'Well – no, I didn't actually mean—'

'Because if Sally is too sweet to receive what she clearly deserves, then perhaps you are prepared to prevent her suffering by taking her place?'

213

'No, I—' Belinda knew she was being manoeuvred into a trap, but the man was too slippery for her.

'Because such a magnanimous display of human kindness would be a joy to behold, and would demonstrate that you are truly a sincere young lady…' his thin smile vanished as he hissed, 'and not just a fake!'

Belinda was cornered. She looked at Sally's innocent face, so full of expectation and gratitude, and her heart melted. This was a chance to atone for all her sins; for her life of vice. And it certainly wouldn't be a beating in the same class as her other noble sacrifice at the fort. 'Very well,' she said. 'If I must.'

Sally brightened at once. 'Thank you,' she gushed. 'And afterwards I will help you with whatever it was you wanted,' which didn't really cheer Belinda at all, given that all she wanted were some directions.

The man wheezed unhealthily and suddenly became a hyperactive blur. 'Sally, you are reprieved but you are not excused. Lower the window blinds; I'll need absolute privacy to savour this beauty at my leisure,' he instructed as he sifted through his drawers of stock. With his head buried he pointed vaguely. 'Then get her over to the chair.' Straps and belts flew over his shoulders and onto the worn floorboards. Belinda wished she hadn't been quite so heroic.

Eventually he straightened up with an evil glint in his lifeless eyes. He was holding a particularly broad and supple belt. He held the brown leather and gazed upon it with a reverence bordering on mad obsession. He made Belinda's skin crawl.

He approached Belinda and Sally and sat in the chair that was there for the convenience of customers. 'Come here,' he commanded, and parted his knees so that Belinda could shuffle between them. He laid the

214

belt across the apparent bulge in his lap, leaned forward a little to lift her skirt at the back, and slipped his hands inside. He gripped her calves, and his touch was as insipid and clammy as she had anticipated. She suppressed a shudder, sensing his volatility and not wanting to incur his true wrath. 'You see, the trouble is,' he explained matter-of-factly as he fumbled slowly up the backs of her legs and admired the rise and fall of her extremely impressive bosom, 'that Sally is inattentive in her work, and I just will not tolerate that.'

Belinda held her tongue. She desperately wanted to voice her opinion of the lizard but feared for Sally's safety. One hand mauled her buttocks while the other groped around to the front. He kicked her feet and manoeuvred her until she stood astride his knees, and then without finesse or consideration he inserted a bony finger up into her vagina. She closed her eyes to the humiliation, more than aware that her juices immediately anointed his loathsome digit. She heard him wheeze and giggle triumphantly.

'My, my... you are a dirty one,' he goaded. 'I think you like the feel of a man – and from what I saw earlier, I think you also like the feel of a woman.' Despite his total lack of any expertise Belinda feared her legs would buckle, such was the height of her arousal first ignited by Sally. The suggestion that she be coupled with the lovely girl to entertain him only served to fuel that arousal. 'Sally's a dirty one too, you know. That's another reason I have to punish her – because she's too free with her affections.'

'That is not true, sir,' Sally ventured.

'Silence!' he spat. 'How dare you speak without permission?'

Belinda could not hide her loathing of the

215

hypocritical lizard any longer. 'Do you not think,' she said whilst staring straight ahead so she didn't have to look at him, 'that you are too harsh with Sally?' She sensed the girl stiffen beside her, and the clawing fingers stilled.

'My dear young lady,' he hissed. 'Do not presume to tell me my business, and I will not presume to tell you yours!' he shook his head. 'Do you have no respect?' But before Belinda could answer him honestly he was holding the belt and addressing his ward. 'Sally, over the counter with this outspoken hussy. Remove the skirt and then place her as you know I like it!'

Without hesitation – the lack of which disappointed Belinda – Sally obeyed her guardian's every order with due diligence. When Belinda was bent over with her cheek pressed to the smooth wood he stood and approached. Belinda heard his boots squeaking in the breathless hush; it would have been comical under any other circumstances. Suddenly her wrists were seized, yanked behind her back so viciously she squealed with the shock, and tied together by another belt before she could resist in any way. The leather bit into her flesh. Her shoulders burned and the position forced her hips, breasts and cheek harder against the uncomfortable counter.

It was not long before his clammy mauling returned to her upthrust buttocks. They were stretched apart and a finger entered her rectum without ceremony. It withdrew almost immediately, and then slipped into her vagina again. It was obvious to Belinda that he had no idea how to stimulate a girl, and it was equally obvious that he considered it an irrelevance.

'Very nice,' he mumbled thoughtfully. 'I will look forward to visiting these two charming little orifices in due course.' He stepped away and Belinda heard the leather belt creaking. It was being wrapped around a fist. 'Sally,' he spoke again. 'Come, stand just behind me.'

'Yes sir,' she whispered obediently.

'You know what to do.'

'Yes sir,' she whispered again. There was a rustle of clothing – and then silence.

As the belt cracked into Belinda she jolted against the counter. The pain she had anticipated was not really forthcoming; she'd certainly had worse. The belt struck again... and again, in time with a slow wet squelching sound. Belinda knew what was occurring; Sally was masturbating her guardian as Belinda was thrashed. She could just imagine the lovely girl reaching around his scrawny waist and pumping his abominable penis in her dainty fists. Much sooner than Belinda expected the belt was thrown to the ground, and she realised the punishment was just a prelude to the main event, or perhaps the obscene creature had little stamina and had got himself too worked up.

'Get the linseed,' he croaked. Sally skittered around the shop. Belinda tensed as oil was dribbled between her buttocks. Her fingers clenched and unclenched anxiously. Her feet were nudged apart, an insistent plum pressed against her anus, and then it popped inside. The lizard hissed and sank deeper, and then Belinda's latter assessment of the situation was confirmed as he squealed and filled her insides before she even had the chance to get accustomed to his invasion.

'Oh yes... that was very nice,' he mumbled. 'Very nice indeed.' Belinda could not agree. 'I like your new friend, Sally,' he continued. 'You must invite her here again. Perhaps next time she could stay the night. We could all share my bed, then we could have some real fun.'

Not a hope in hell, thought Belinda, but held her tongue. She tried to relax the strain on her bent and taut body, but then she felt the plum at her normal entrance and tensed again. Surely he wasn't ready to take her again. Perhaps she had been wrong about his stamina. He may not last very long, but he certainly seemed to have an admirable recovery rate, and the rigid column that proceeded to forge its way deep into her vagina proved that beyond doubt. This time he had more control, and as his thighs slapped rhythmically against Belinda's she felt her traitorous excitement mounting and mounting.

'The belt...' Belinda heard. 'Pull the belt.' And then dainty hands pulled back on the leather that bound her wrists and she moaned at the pain as her torso lifted from the counter. Bony hands reached round and cupped her vulnerable breasts through the blouse. Her nipples poked through the material into the sweaty palms as her soft mounds of flesh were squashed back into her chest. Belinda's head lolled forward and her silky hair swept the counter. Her muscles gripped the reaming stalk. She ground her bottom back against the man. His breathing became more ragged, and then they erupted together. Through waves of delight Belinda hated herself; she was a shameful hussy – the man had been right.

For another hour or so the lizard continued to indulge himself with Belinda's fine body, with Sally's assistance. As he did so, and whilst in a most bizarre position, he told the two young ladies that he desired nothing more than to see them together, but that he would save that special treat for Belinda's next visit, which, he had little doubt, would not be too long in the future. Then he could prepare for their long night together accordingly. Belinda shuddered at the thought and wondered how he could be so confident of her return. When he had finally satisfied his lusts Belinda was allowed to go out into the yard and wash herself under the pump. When she went back inside and dressed she told them she was looking for Albert Hopeworth, and her distaste for the man only increased when he giggled insanely and became coarsely abusive about her uncle, but without giving any specific reasons. It was Sally who told her she would find him up at the church, and Belinda then realised why the lizard harboured such hatred; her uncle was obviously as virtuous as he was despicable, and she was happy for that.

The streets were still empty when she left the dingy shop and headed for the church. She could feel the beady eyes crawling over every inch of her as she went. After thirty or forty yards she turned to wave to Sally. They were standing in the doorway, and he had an arm around her shoulder and one hand stuffed possessively down the front of her dress, where it blatantly toyed with her lovely bosom. He leered and shouted after her, 'You won't get any pleasure from your uncle, you know! When you want some real fun you just come right along back here and see me! I'll be waiting! D'you hear?'

Chapter Fifteen

Belinda followed the churchyard wall until she found the squeaky iron gate. A woman in black with a couple of children was just leaving. She looked as if she would be unlikely to understand English, so Belinda simply pointed in through the gate, raised her eyebrows, and said clearly and slowly, 'Albert Hopeworth?'

To her relief the woman's life-weary face brightened, and with a warm smile she nodded and pointed in the same direction.

'Oh thank you!' sang Belinda joyously.

'De nada,' said the woman.

'I'm sorry?' said Belinda, in case she had missed something important.

The woman sighed. 'You say thank you – I say de nada,' she said in stilted English. 'It is like you say in your language; that is all right, don't mention it.'

'Oh, I'm sorry,' apologised Belinda, recognising the accent and secretly admiring the woman for at least attempting a foreign tongue. 'I don't speak Spanish,' she said humbly. After exchanging polite smiles the woman hurried the children through the gates and was gone.

The place was deserted except for another woman replacing flowers at an old grave and a priest chatting to a couple of filthy gravediggers who were leaning heavily on their shovels.

'Albert Hopeworth?' she asked the woman, who nodded, smiled cordially and pointed to the priest. Belinda could not believe it. Not only had she found her uncle, but he was an honourable man of the cloth!

All those months of misery and danger had not been in vain after all. A brand new life lay ahead of Belinda Hopeworth, a life she richly deserved.

She ran as fast as her aching back and legs would let her. As she approached the priest turned to see whom it was shrieking like a lunatic and breaking the tranquillity of his graveyard. He was a large man of a few years over fifty. He had an intelligent and cultured face. He studied her closely as she neared, as if he vaguely recognised her features but couldn't place them.

'Uncle Albert Hopeworth!' she shrieked with joy.

'Er, er yes…?' he said uncertainly.

'I'm your niece from Liverpool… Belinda!'

'But—'

'Oh uncle!' she threw her arms around the bewildered clergyman's neck. The two gravediggers grinned at each other and spat tobacco juice onto the ground in quick succession. This could prove to be highly embarrassing for their employer. What had he been up to then? With him somewhat flustered and distracted they took the opportunity to assess the form of the bubbly new arrival. From the glint in their eyes it was clear they were suitably impressed.

'No – wait,' stammered the priest, trying to prise away the arms that threatened to throttle him. 'I'm not your uncle… he's over there.'

'Where?' Belinda turned and looked around, still grinning from ear to ear. 'Where is he?'

The priest suddenly realised what was happening, and placed a comforting hand on her shoulder. The same realization fell on the gravediggers, and with an uncomfortable cough they turned away and found something to dig.

'It would seem I have some unfortunate news for

221

you, my child,' said the priest as kindly as he could.

'Why?' The smile on her beautiful face flickered a little uncertainly for the first time. 'What sort of unfortunate news?'

'You're a little late.' The priest pointed at a freshly dug and bare grave. 'He's there. We buried him only this morning.' He shook his head and dabbed a crisp linen hanky to his balding pate. 'The first funeral ever performed here without a single mourner.'

Belinda looked at the priest with utter disbelief in her wide eyes, looked back at the grave, and fainted.

When she came to on the priest's sofa she felt sick with the memory of why she had fainted in the first place. All her trials and tribulations since leaving Liverpool had been in vain. She wanted to scream and shout, but merely lay passively as a rather severe-looking housekeeper gave her warm milk and biscuits. The priest was watching her closely from an armchair.

'I hate to tell you this now, Belinda, but you have a right to know,' he said once she had finished the little snack. 'Your uncle was a bad man. He was a bully, he drank far too much, and he accumulated heavy gambling debts to characters who held an extremely dim view of his behaviour...'

Belinda shook her head sadly as the priest told her more and more.

'...Unfortunately, rightly or wrongly, I tried to help by loaning him church funds. Whether the money or my faith in him would ever have been repaid I somehow doubt, and now we'll never know – he got himself murdered in the local saloon two nights ago. He obviously hadn't used the loan to repay his creditors.'

'How was he murdered?' she asked timidly, not

really sure if she wanted to know.

'Shot in the back of the head.'

'Who did it? Have the authorities caught him?'

'An unknown killer, probably on a contract. It was inevitable, I suppose.'

'This is terrible,' said Belinda.

'It is terrible,' agreed the priest. 'And now my concern is that if word gets out about your arrival here the perpetrators of this heinous crime will be looking for you next.'

'No – surely not!' Belinda shivered with fear. 'I have nothing to do with my uncle's debts!'

'They may not see it that way,' he said gravely. 'I therefore propose that you remain here until things have settled down a little.'

'But what about your friends and parishioners? They'll wonder who I am.'

'I have considered that,' continued the priest smoothly. 'We'll tell them you are my niece from England.' He watched Belinda eye the housekeeper. 'Don't worry about Mrs Privett – she's as trustworthy as the day is long.'

'I don't know what to say,' said Belinda with immense relief. 'How can I ever thank you?'

'Ah,' the priest raised a forefinger to indicate the discussion wasn't yet over, 'that brings me on to the next matter; the matter of repaying the church funds.'

'It does?' Belinda didn't like the sound of that too much.

'As your uncle's only next of kin in America there is much you can do to contribute.'

'There is?'

'There is,' he nodded. 'I think it is only right that whilst you remain here you work off his considerable debt to the church.'

Belinda considered this. She had nowhere else to go. Her life could be in grave danger if she left this sanctuary. She had no other choice but to agree. 'Very well,' she said. 'What will I have to do?'

'Anything as I see fit,' said the priest as he dabbed his extensive brow again and crossed his legs.

'I'll begin first thing in the morning,' she said.

'I think you'd better begin right now,' he said, and surreptitiously eased the pressure building beneath his cassock. 'Because you see, my dear, I also feel it only right that someone should accept the punishment for your uncle's wrongdoing, and as he isn't here, that responsibility also falls on you.'

'Oh,' said Belinda. She wasn't so sure about that – but then perhaps he had a point. Her uncle had clearly wronged the church, and for that someone should pay; family honour was at stake. She lowered her gaze to the plush carpet and nodded.

'Good,' said the priest, as he took the opportunity to gaze longingly upon the highly promising undulations hiding inside the white blouse. 'Mrs Privett,' he addressed his housekeeper without taking his eyes from the appetising morsel lying on his sofa. 'Kindly fetch my cane from the desk drawer, and then you may leave us. I will not be accepting visitors for the rest of the day.'